TORTILLAS
AND SECOND
CHANCES

Other books by Sylvia Renfro:

Poppy's Place

TORTILLAS AND SECOND CHANCES

•

Sylvia Renfro

AVALON BOOKS
NEW YORK

Published by Thomas Bouregy & Co., Inc.
160 Madison Avenue, New York, NY 10016

Library of Congress Cataloging-in-Publication Data

Renfro, Sylvia.
    Tortillas and second chances / Sylvia Renfro.
        p. cm.
    ISBN 978-0-8034-9833-4 (acid-free paper)
    I. Title.

PS3618.E576T67 2007
813'.6—dc22

                                            2007003745

PRINTED IN THE UNITED STATES OF AMERICA
ON ACID-FREE PAPER
BY HADDON CRAFTSMEN, BLOOMSBURG, PENNSYLVANIA

In memory of Carol Messacar, RN, whose skill, compassion, and generosity touched many, many lives.

With special thanks to my friends in Needles, California: Jimbo and Cathy McConnell for sharing their exciting stories about life on the professional boat racing circuit; Kenny Baldwin, who let me hang out at Premier Sports; and the staff at Needles Desert Communities Hospital, where I learned that healing and humor frequently go hand in hand. Sometimes, you just gotta laugh!

Last but not least, a big hug to my mom, Virginia Husk, who taught for many years in the Needles schools, and who taught me to love animals, children, and a good book.

Chapter One

*H*air *as black as a raven's wing.*

It couldn't be. Not after all these years. Celeste Nilson Walker closed her eyes, willing the image to disappear.

When she opened them, he stood in the doorway of the hospital cafeteria. A summer shirt revealed the burnished skin of his throat and forearms, and heavy-lidded dark eyes stared straight into her soul.

Ray Fontana.

Celeste bumped into something unyielding and realized too late that the doctor in front of her had stopped dead in his tracks. Her tray tilted upward and orange gelatin slid against her chest. Cherry tomatoes bounced around the cafeteria like crazy balls.

"*Santos benditos!*" Holy Saints! Struggling to

1

catch her daughter's plate, Celeste lost her own. It hit the floor with a resounding crash.

The room seemed to freeze in time. The clink and clatter of silverware, the scraping of chairs, the hum of lunchtime conversation, all ceased. Even the cafeteria ladies stopped ladling food onto plates.

Mia's seven-year-old voice broke the silence. "I'm glad I didn't do that!"

As the lunchtime crowd erupted in laughter, several women ran to take Celeste's tray and wipe at her ruined blouse. Cafeteria workers brought wet towels to mop up the spilled salad. Celeste apologized profusely to Dr. Bandini, who seemed more surprised than injured by the incident.

When she looked again toward the cafeteria entrance, Ray was gone.

Taking Mia's hand, she headed for the back door of the cafeteria and the employee parking lot. "Looks like it's peanut butter and jelly sandwiches for us today."

"That's okay. I like PB&Js better than salad anyway," said Mia.

Celeste looked into big blue-gray eyes, so like her own, and gave her daughter's hand a squeeze. "Thanks, sweetie."

Then, glancing around the room to be sure no one was watching, she grabbed a shaker from the closest table and threw salt over her left shoulder. With Ray

Fontana back in town, she'd need all the good luck she could get.

Ray leaned against the cool white wall of the hospital corridor. His heart was pounding, the blood thundering through his veins. He hadn't felt so much adrenaline since his boat racing days.

He'd thought of Celeste through the years. Often. When he looked out the floor-to-ceiling window of his condo in Bal Harbor the changing moods of the ocean reminded him of Celeste's eyes. She was his first love, maybe the only woman he had ever truly loved. Like the rest of his life in Aubrey's Landing, he'd left her far behind.

He belonged in Miami Beach now, in a world of fast cars, faster boats, beautiful women, and high finance. Or at least, he'd managed to buy his way into that life. Money and power had made him a popular, if not universally beloved, man.

Why was he so shaken by this tall, awkward blond with ramrod posture and forbiddingly stiff hair? He preferred his women soft and voluptuous. Receptive. There was certainly nothing receptive about Celeste. She looked about as warm as a snow cone.

Ray smiled at the memory of his favorite childhood treat. He hadn't thought about snow cones for years. Nothing like coming home to stir up the ghosts of your past.

Celeste looked like she'd seen one of those ghosts when she spotted him in the doorway.

Ray pushed off from the wall and headed down the corridor toward the Acute Care floor. Celeste's reaction pleased him somehow. He wondered, had she thought about him too?

Gus was sitting up in bed when Ray entered, eating what appeared to be creamed chipped beef on toast. They'd had a more descriptive name for it at the Arizona Boys Ranch. His old friend wore a disgusted scowl as he poked at the gluey white substance on his plate. That was a good sign. For the first couple of days after his heart attack, Gus had been too weak to show any of his characteristic feistiness.

"Hey, old man. What's the matter? You don't like what's on the menu?" He sat in the chair beside Gus' bed.

"I'd just as soon eat a cow puck. Gol durn hospitals. They lock you up and then try to poison you. I wouldn't be surprised if the dang die-tician was getting a kickback from the mortuary." He tossed his fork onto the plate.

Ray's lips twitched as he tried not to grin. Gus was definitely feeling better. "Don't worry. When you get out of here, I'll buy you the biggest steak in town."

"That ain't the worst of it. The doc tells me I have to change my whole life when they spring me from this place. They want to get me into their cardiac rehab program so they can teach me about exercising and eating a low-fat diet." Gus spat out the last three words like a mouthful of slimy worms.

"Then we'll make it a lean steak and a salad. Did they say when you'll be going home?"

"The doc wants to keep me a few more days to make sure I'm stable. Then I'll have to hook up with a home health care nurse for a while. I hope she's a looker." Gus winked at him. "Speaking of lookers, an old friend of yours visited me this morning."

"Let me guess." Ray put his fingertips to his forehead and closed his eyes for a moment. "Celeste Nilson."

"Yep. Only it's Celeste Nilson Walker now. She's the social services director for the hospital. How'd you know?"

"She saw me in the cafeteria and spilled a tray of food all over herself." He smiled at the recollection of Celeste, with orange gelatin dripping from her blouse and a look of pure horror on her face. Women had reacted to him strongly in the past, but never quite like that.

"Is that so?" Gus' face took on a speculative look. "If a woman like Celeste spilled her tray on account of me, I'd take it as a compliment. You two were sweet on each other once, weren't you?"

Ray felt the old bitterness surge inside him.

More ghosts of the past. He kept his voice neutral. "That was a long time ago. Doc Nilson didn't think I was suitable match for his only daughter."

Gus looked at him with keen eyes and nodded. "Old Doc Nilson had a stroke a couple of years ago. Celeste moved back to Aubrey's Landing to be close to him. She's single again, you know. Raising a child by herself."

"I saw the little girl in the cafeteria. She has her mother's eyes." Clear gray eyes, with a hint of blue. Eyes that changed with the weather or her mood or the clothes she wore. Ray was silent for a moment, remembering how those eyes had looked at him with such love and trust.

In another lifetime, Celeste had believed in him, more than he believed in himself. All it had taken was a few well-chosen words from Doc Nilson, words calculated to play on Ray's insecurities, to make him run. Later, when he realized what he had given up, it was too late.

Ray brushed aside his regrets. Dr. Nilson had been right. Celeste's love for him was a childish fantasy. It wouldn't have withstood the rigors of life on the professional boat racing circuit. Hell, she hadn't even finished a semester at college before she found someone else.

She'd been raised for a life of comfort and privilege. What had gone wrong? Ray wondered. Why did she look so tense and thin? It seemed Celeste's life hadn't worked out exactly as Dr. Nilson had planned.

Gus' raspy voice cut through his reverie. "I've been thinking, Ray. About what I'm gonna do when I get out. The doc says I have to take it easy for a while and, well, I was wondering if you might like to stick around and run the boat shop for me. I'd pay you, of course."

He held up a hand as Ray started to protest. "Oh, I know you don't need the money, but you sure as heck could use a vacation. You could spend a little time with your brother." Gus paused, watching him with twinkling blue eyes. "Maybe even spark an old flame. What do you say, Ray? It'll only be for a couple of weeks, until I can hire someone. I'd consider it a personal favor."

Ray regarded his friend with amusement. The old man was still looking out for him, in his own peculiar way. He owed Gus more than he could repay in one lifetime, and the old coyote knew it. His business in Miami would have to wait.

"Sure, Gus. You know I will. Only don't get your hopes up about me and Celeste Nilson Walker." His voice took on a prissy tone as he pronounced her name. "She's a little too uptight for my taste—all elbows and raw nerves. She might as well hang a Keep Off sign around her neck."

"The woman I saw this morning wasn't all elbows." Gus shoved the tray away and settled back against the pillows. "But then my eyesight ain't what it used to be. I'm glad you're coming to work for me again, Ray. It'll be like old times." With a satisfied smile, he closed his eyes and drifted off.

Like old times. Ray rose from the uncomfortable vinyl-covered visitor chair and gazed down at Gus. The old man snored softly. A faint rose color had replaced the ashen gray in his cheeks. Ray was glad to see his friend looking better.

Gus was more than a friend, really. He'd been like a father to Ray. Certainly more of a father than Alonso Fontana. When Al wasn't in jail, he was railing against the injustice of life in one of the local taverns. Or intimidating his wife and sons.

More ghosts. Old times in Aubrey's Landing hadn't been so good for Al Fontana's boy. He was just like his old man. Everyone said so. He looked like Al, moved like him, had the same bad attitude.

Ray had done his best to fulfill the town's expectations. Somehow, as he tottered on the edge of the precipice, just about to tumble in, Gus caught hold of him and pulled him back.

No doubt about it. He owed Gus. And although he wouldn't admit it, he was more than a little curious about Celeste. The woman stirred feelings in him, feelings he thought had died a long time ago. He liked it, he decided. He liked the jolt she gave him, the surge of adrenaline.

Ray whistled "Luck Be a Lady Tonight" as he

walked out into the September heat. He headed across the visitor's parking lot toward a shiny green rental car. From its vantage point high on a hill, Aubrey's Landing Medical Center had an enviable view of the Colorado River Valley. In the distance, the blue ribbon of river wound through emerald fields of cotton and alfalfa.

Two weeks in Aubrey's Landing, he thought as he unlocked the door and slid behind the wheel. He hadn't spent more than two days here since he left eight years ago.

He turned onto the main street and headed toward his hotel on the edge of town. The place had grown considerably since the last time he'd been here. His vision dimmed as he recalled the circumstances of that visit. Gas stations and fast food joints sped past the car windows, unnoticed.

His boat racing career had ended, leaving him with a high school education and few prospects. Losing his mom was the final blow. He felt like the last piece of his heart had been ripped from his chest.

Then he'd seen Doc Nilson standing in the rear of the church during the funeral. Their eyes met for a brief moment. In that instant, Ray read hatred, and satisfaction. His life had turned out just as the doctor had predicted.

Something clicked inside him. He made up his mind to do whatever it took to become a success. His father might have been a drunken, no-account loser but he'd be damned if he'd follow in Al's footsteps. He'd taken his mechanical aptitude and knowledge of boat racing and turned it into a multi-million-dollar business.

Let them believe whatever they wanted, Ray decided. Let them think he was a failure. A good boat mechanic but only a flash-in-the-pan driver. As far as the citizens of Aubrey's Landing were concerned, he was just a regular guy in town to help an old friend.

The more he thought about it, the more Ray liked the idea. He hadn't kept in touch with anyone from Aubrey's Landing but Gus and his brother, Micah. Both men understood he wanted the details of his life kept strictly confidential.

When he stepped out of the spotlight of the professional boat racing circuit, Ray found he'd lost his taste for publicity. His business dealings were discreet, his relationships with women unencumbered by love or commitment. That's the way he liked it, and the way he intended to keep it.

Right now he had a few errands to run. He pulled into the parking lot of a chain discount store. The large American flag in front reminded him that it was Labor Day, almost eight years to the day since he'd left Celeste and Aubrey's Landing behind. Life wasn't without its irony.

First, he'd buy some appropriate clothes for a working man. Then, back to the hotel to call his secretary at Native Spirit Boats and tell her to clear his calendar for the next couple of weeks. Poor Mavis would tear her hair out, but she'd manage.

Finally, he thought he'd pay a visit to his big brother. If anyone could fill him in on Celeste, it was the Reverend Micah Fontana.

"Mama, who was that man at the hospital?"

Celeste straightened Mia's bedclothes, buying time. She'd been dreading this moment and had hoped she could put it off a little longer. "What man, darling?"

"The man who was staring at you, just before you dropped our food."

Okay, she couldn't avoid it. She sat on the edge of Mia's bed. "He's someone I knew a long time ago."

"Was he your friend?"

Celeste chose her words with care. "He was my friend once. Sometimes friends disappoint each other. I haven't seen him for years."

Mia digested this information, a serious expression on her small, pale face. "Is he a nice man?"

"Yes, I think so. At least he was when I knew him. He's Reverend Micah's brother, you know."

Mia's expression brightened at the mention of Micah's name. "He *is*? He must be nice then."

The scales had definitely tipped in Ray's favor, Celeste thought. She kissed her daughter on the forehead, inhaling the fresh clean scent of Mia's shampoo. "That's enough questions for tonight, sweetie. Time to go to sleep."

"Mama?"

Celeste paused at the door. "Yes, darling?"

"Why did he . . . disappoint you?"

She looked at her daughter, propped on one elbow on blue and white sheets, illumined by the glow of a teddy bear night-light. A wave of tenderness engulfed her. "It's a long story and it would be difficult for a little girl to understand. I'll tell you when you're older," she answered.

"But I'm already seven and a half!"

"Good night, Mia. I love you."

Mia's sigh held an exasperated note. "Good night, Mom. I love you too."

Celeste padded to the kitchen and ran cold water in her stainless steel teapot. She needed to treat herself to a few minutes of tranquility. It had been *un día monstro,* as Rosa would say. A monstrous day.

Going to the antique oak hutch, she lovingly ran her hand over its glossy finish. The hutch, dining room table, and chairs were part of her inheritance from her mother. Sometimes, sitting at the table on a quiet evening, she imagined feeling Alice's presence in the room.

She had few clear memories of her mother, only the stories Rosa had told her. Since she'd been old enough to remember, Rosa Martinez had been their cook, live-in housekeeper, and her *mamacita*, little mama.

She peered through the beveled glass doors of the hutch at her collection of china cups and saucers. Some were old and quite expensive, others valuable only to her. She needed something special tonight. A cup as delicate as first love.

Celeste silently scolded herself. *You've been reading too many romance novels.* Opening the door of the hutch, she selected a white cup and saucer, edged in gold, with a hand-painted pink rose on the side.

Later, cup of steaming chamomile tea in hand, she looked at the blueprints for the new Obstetrics Center spread on the table in front of her. She'd accepted a seat on the planning committee last year.

The hoping committee would be more accurate, she thought, flipping through plans as she sipped the hot tea.

Two comfortably furnished birthing suites, an office, and an examination room. They'd had trouble finding the financing for even this modest beginning. The project had taken up most of her free time, but it would all be worthwhile if, no, *when* they succeeded in building the Obstetrics Center for low-income families.

She'd seen far too many women arrive in the emergency room to give birth with little or no prenatal care. Some were the wives of farm workers from Parker Valley, south of Aubrey's Landing. Others were frightened, unmarried girls. All seemed ignorant of the dangers posed to themselves and their babies by poor nutrition and inadequate medical care.

Celeste understood their fear and feeling of isolation. As Rosa was fond of saying, she'd walked in their sandals.

She thought for a moment about how her life had changed in the last few years. It hadn't been an easy road but she was proud of her accomplishments. They lived in a nice little house she'd paid for herself. She served the community through her work at the hospital and on the obstetrics center board. And she had Mia, the most wonderful gift God had given her.

God and Ray Fontana.

Chapter Two

"Shall we gather at the river, Where bright angel feet have trod; With its crystal tide forever, Flowing by the throne of God? . . ."

Ray sat in the back corner of Aubrey's Landing Community Church. He closed his eyes and let the music wash over him. Even now, he could pick out Celeste's sweet, soaring soprano. The first time he heard her voice, he thought she was an angel. When he looked up in the choir loft and saw her innocent young face framed by shining blond hair, he was sure. No one who looked and sounded so beautiful could be mortal.

As the Rev. Micah Fontana settled in at the pulpit, Ray experienced an uneasy feeling of déjà vu. He'd never had much use for religion, still didn't.

But here he was again, hoping for a chance to speak with Celeste. Or, failing that, just wanting to hear her voice.

He hadn't been able to get her out of his mind since their chance encounter at the hospital. Micah had not been at all helpful. In fact, he'd invoked his clergyman's confidentiality on the subject, saying he couldn't discuss Celeste's personal life without her permission. Ray briefly wondered if Micah was interested in Celeste himself, but quickly dismissed the idea. His brother's only interest in women was as members of his flock.

Ray shifted uncomfortably in the pew. The new blue jeans he'd purchased were stiff and he felt ridiculous in a plaid cotton dress shirt and nubby beige tie. He glanced around at the other male members of the congregation. Most had dressed for the weather in cotton slacks and open collared shirts.

At least he could lose the tie. He pulled off the neckpiece as discreetly as possible. There. Now he wouldn't look like quite such a nerd.

On the other hand, he didn't want to appear too sophisticated either. Designer street wear and Italian loafers wouldn't project the working man's image he sought.

Up in front, Micah went through the familiar motions of the service. Ray rose and sat with the rest of the congregation but his mind floated like the dust motes caught in the golden glow of sunlight through stained glass.

He'd been twenty-six years old the first time he heard Celeste sing. A world-class competitor, he'd won Formula One boat races in South Africa, Berlin, Milan, and London. It had been a long time since he visited Aubrey's Landing, and even longer since he'd set foot in a church. He came to please his mom, Juleska.

Yeah, he'd been on top of the world then. He even dared to think he had a chance with Doctor Nilson's daughter.

The Reverend Fontana announced another hymn. Ray didn't bother to open the hymnal, listening instead for the sweet, clear tones of Celeste's voice. He'd fallen in love before he ever saw her. Even now, he felt the cold, hard case around his heart begin to crack a little.

All these emotions, in a man who prided himself on not having any, Ray thought. It should be an interesting couple of weeks.

Later, when he filed out into the sunshine with the rest of the congregation, he spotted Celeste and her daughter chatting with another woman and child. Celeste's back was to him but the two little girls watched him with bright, curious eyes. He smiled and held a forefinger to his lips as he approached.

Just before he reached her, Celeste became aware of the girls' rapt looks in his direction. Or maybe she felt his presence. She spun around and, for an instant, he saw fear in her eyes. Immediately, she drew herself up, clutching her purse a little tighter. A curtain descended over her features. Ray knew that look well, the nothing-you-say-or-do-can-touch-me look. He'd practiced it for years.

"Hello, Celeste."

She stood eye-to-eye with him in high heels, her gaze as cold as the Potomac in February. "Ray."

She looked good in a simple aqua dress. The modest, knee-length hem couldn't hide those miles of legs. "How have you been?" he asked.

"Recently? Or for the past eight years?"

There was no mistaking the enmity in her clipped and chilly tone. The petite blond Celeste had been chatting with stepped forward to break the tension.

"You must be Ray Fontana. I've heard so much about you," she said, offering her hand.

Ray shook it. "Some of it good, I hope." He cast a sideways glance at Celeste's stiff posture and un-smiling countenance.

"Of course. Reverend Micah speaks of you often. And the whole town knows about your boat racing career. You're something of a local legend. Oh, my name's Patti Kowalski. I'm the activities director at the recreation center. This is my daughter, Rowena."

Ray reached down to take the child's hand. She

was a cute little thing, with curly blond hair and thick round glasses. "Ah, the fair Rowena. She was the queen of love and beauty in *Ivanhoe*."

Rowena's plump, freckled face lit up. She smiled, revealing a dimple in her right cheek. "You read *Ivanhoe*?"

"Only about a hundred times. It was my favorite book when I was a kid."

"Me too." She beamed at him. "Mom and I have been reading it at bedtime."

Ray turned toward the other girl. She was a head shorter than Rowena and a couple of years younger. An unusual child, not pretty exactly, but striking, with straight dark bangs that accentuated her high cheekbones. Thick, shiny hair, the color of dark chocolate, fell to the middle of her back. The child was too thin, almost fragile looking. There was something about her he couldn't quite put his finger on, something oddly familiar. He stooped in front of her. "And who are you?"

Big gray eyes stared at him. Her mother's eyes. Before the child could answer, Celeste stepped closer and put a protective arm around her. "This is my daughter, Mia."

"Hello, Mia. That's a pretty name. It means *mine* in Spanish."

"I know." Mia didn't smile but continued to watch him appraisingly. She'd be a tougher sell than Rowena but Ray had no doubt he could win her over.

He'd enjoyed working with the younger children at the boys' ranch. Those kids could spot a phony a mile away, but if you treated them with kindness and respect, they'd give it back a hundredfold.

"We have to go." Celeste grasped Mia's hand. "See you tonight, Patti."

"We'll be there."

Left alone with Ray, Patti fidgeted with her purse. Obviously, Celeste hadn't filled her in on their past relationship. All the better. Maybe he could enlist her help.

"What's going on tonight?" Ray asked.

"The church social. It's held once a month. Everyone brings a main course and the church provides dessert. It's homemade ice cream this month."

"Sounds great. What time does it start?"

"Usually people start eating about six thirty. You're welcome to come. There's always more than enough food."

"I just might do that." Ray gazed at Celeste's retreating back. She was walking so fast, Mia had to trot to keep up. He watched as she buckled the little girl into an older model car. Not what he'd expect Dr. Nilson's daughter to drive.

"Well then, I guess we'll be going too. It was nice meeting you," Patti said.

"My pleasure. Bye, Lady Rowena." He bowed slightly and was rewarded with a delighted giggle.

"Good-bye, Mr. Fontana."

Ray remained standing on the sidewalk as Celeste drove past the church. Mia watched him with big, fascinated eyes until they were out of sight.

"Been a long time since I've seen you in church, Ray. You wouldn't have some special reason for attending this morning, would you?"

Ray turned. Micah towered over him, smiling benignly in the sunlight. Once again Ray was struck by the differences between them. At thirty-six, his lanky, blue-eyed brother looked more like a choir boy than a minister. Ray, on the other hand, had never looked like a choir boy. Or behaved like one.

"I came to hear you preach, big brother."

Micah shook his head. "I'll bet you can't tell me the subject of my sermon. No matter. I'm happy to see you here, for whatever reason. Why don't you wait in the office while I change? I'll take you to lunch."

"That sounds good. And the subject of your sermon was the beatitudes. Although I thought the return of the prodigal son would have been more appropriate."

Ray wandered around his brother's office while he waited, stopping now and then to pick up a trinket or examine the framed certificates on the wall. A big oak desk occupied one corner of the room. Next to the desk stood a filing cabinet. A couch, coffee table, and two overstuffed chairs filled the opposite side of the office.

His gaze returned to the four-drawer filing cabinet. What kind of records would a church keep? He drew closer to inspect the labels on each drawer: *Baptismal Records, A–G, H–Q, R–Z* in descending order. The bottom drawer read Correspondence.

Nothing too exciting. A flicker of motion drew his attention to the window. Outside, in the grassy courtyard, a couple of kids played on a swing set. Their mothers sat in the shade of a cottonwood tree and talked. He heard Micah enter through a side door.

"That's our new preschool." Micah pointed to the building directly behind the church. "The one you paid for. I was hoping to give you a tour. It's been a godsend for the working parents in this community."

Ray turned away from the window. "No need. I'm sure you did a fine job. All I ask is that my contribution remain anonymous." He hooked his thumbs in the belt loops of his too-stiff jeans and hitched them up slightly. "As far as the citizens of Aubrey's Landing are concerned, I'm just a regular guy."

Micah looked him up and down, a slight smile tugging at his lips. "I can see you've dressed for the part. I don't understand your reluctance to be acknowledged for your good works, but I'll respect your wishes."

"Good. Where do we eat?"

Micah hesitated. "I thought we'd go to Betty's. For old times' sake."

The ghosts of Aubrey's Landing. From the look on Micah's face, Ray could tell he sensed them too. Ray's homecoming had awakened old hurts, pain, and regret. He promised Gus he'd stay for two weeks. He might as well face his demons.

Ray's mouth twisted in a mirthless smile. "Lead on, big brother."

The place hadn't changed much in the half-dozen years he'd been away. Although the booths and counter stools boasted new red vinyl uphol-stery, the black-and-white tiled floor and long chrome-edged counter looked exactly as he re-membered it. In Miami, the decor would be called fifties retro. In Aubrey's Landing, it was just Betty's Diner.

"I feel like I'm in the Twilight Zone." Ray sipped a cup of coffee. Every booth was filled and several people stood in front of the cash register, waiting to be seated.

The hostess, a member of Micah's congregation, had found them a seat at the counter until a booth opened up. Ray noticed how she fussed over the Reverend Fontana, refilling his coffee, supplying a small pitcher of fresh half-and-half and even pol-ishing his water-spotted teaspoon with her apron.

The woman had done everything but throw herself at his feet. As usual, Micah was oblivious.

"Betty's is a local institution. One of the few constants in this age of change. Remember when mom worked the evening shift? We'd do our homework at that back booth." Micah waved to the family sitting there.

"You did homework. I read novels."

Micah chuckled. "That's right. You always were a voracious reader. And a rebel. Do you still enjoy adventure stories?"

"My tastes run more to nonfiction these days: business, economics, philosophy. I no longer need adventure in my life. Or escapism." Not since he'd escaped from Aubrey's Landing.

"Funny you should say that. It seems to me you're always searching for a new adventure, whether it's taking over another company or developing a newer, faster boat for Native Spirit. You have a restless nature, Ray. Always have. It's probably why you're so successful."

The waitress, a bouncy college-age girl, appeared to seat them. Ray watched as she sashayed down the aisle, adding a little extra swing to her hips.

"You all take your time now. I hope you'll see something you like." She gave Ray a seductive smile as she handed him the menu.

Small-town girls, he thought. She was probably looking for a little excitement, or maybe a ticket out of Aubrey's Landing. "Are the hamburgers still as good as they used to be?" he asked.

"The best in town," the waitress answered.

"Then I won't need a menu. Just bring me a cheeseburger, fries, and a chocolate shake." He looked at Micah. "For old times' sake."

"I'll have the same." Micah handed both menus to the waitress.

"So, tell me, big brother. Why did you bring me here? And don't say it was for the cheeseburgers. I can tell you have something on your mind."

Micah fiddled with his napkin and silverware as a flush colored his cheeks. Poor Micah. Ever since they were boys his fair complexion had given him away. He was uncomfortable about something. Ray waited, although he was pretty sure he knew the reason for his brother's invitation.

Micah stopped fiddling and looked him the eye. "You know I love you, Ray."

"I've never doubted that."

"I know I didn't do right by you and Ma. I was the older brother. I should have taken care of you. Instead, I went to live with Reverend Simpson and his family. I took the easy road and left you and Ma to cope the best you could."

This wasn't at all what he'd expected. "Listen, Micah, that was a long time ago. You were just a kid."

Micah stopped him. "I need to say this. I was ashamed of our family. I was ashamed of Pop for being the town drunk, of you because you were always in trouble, even of Ma, God forgive me. Just because she was poor and uneducated. I didn't realize until I went to seminary what a gem she was . . ." His voice trailed off. "Sometimes I guess you have to go away to appreciate what you've left behind."

The ghosts were swirling around him fast and furiously now. Mom in her waitress uniform, serving up hamburgers; he and Micah, sitting at this very booth, one dark head and one blond, bent over their books. He wanted to hug Micah, tell him he loved him, but the words stuck in his throat. It had been too long since he'd said them to anyone.

"You were a good son, Micah. Mom wanted you to live with the reverend. You know she always wanted what was best for you."

Micah shook his head. "That's what I'm trying to tell you. I wasn't a good son. Or at least not a faithful one. I ran away. You went the distance, Ray. You were the good son."

Ray felt as if an unseen hand squeezed his heart. One week in Aubrey's Landing and his emotions had been stirred more than in the past several years.

The waitress appeared, sparing him the necessity of responding. She lowered the tray of food from her shoulder. "Here you go. Two cheeseburgers, two fries, and two chocolate shakes. Can I get you anything else?" She looked hopefully at Ray.

He maintained eye contact just a little longer than necessary, then gave her a slow smile. "That's all for now."

The girl had provided a welcome distraction. He buried his childhood long ago and had no desire to resurrect it.

What he remembered most was being angry. It seemed like he spent the first fifteen years of his life angry. At Boys Ranch he'd learned to channel his anger into boxing and had won the camp championship two years in a row.

Yeah, he had more guts and intensity than anyone who challenged him, in the boxing ring, on the boat racing circuit, or in the financial arena. He'd achieved every goal, fulfilled every ambition, and still, it wasn't enough. He couldn't shake the feeling of dissatisfaction.

Something was missing from his life.

"Shame on you for flirting with that girl." Micah grinned at him, then took a bite of his burger. The grin was weak and his eyes a little watery. Nevertheless, Ray breathed a sigh of relief.

"I just brightened her day a little. You could have done the same for our hostess. Where's your Christian charity, brother? Or is there a special lady in your life?" He already knew the answer but wanted to get their conversation back on a more comfortable plane. He'd had enough ghosts and confessions for one day.

"You know my work keeps me busy. But since you brought up the subject, what's with you and Celeste? She didn't look too happy after church this morning." Micah threw him a piercing glance before reaching for the ketchup.

Uh-oh. He seemed to have stumbled onto part two of Micah's reason for staging this tête-a-tête. He smiled, deciding to tease his brother a little. "Nothing yet. But I plan to change that in the near future."

Micah didn't return his grin. He set down his burger, then paused for a moment, weighing his words. "Go easy, Ray. Celeste has had some tough breaks. I don't want to see her hurt again."

Ray held his hands up in surrender. "Hey, relax. I was just joking. Anyway, how much damage can I do in a couple of weeks?"

Instead of deterring him, Micah's warning sharpened his curiosity. As did Celeste's reaction to him in the hospital cafeteria, and the fleeting look of fear on her face when she saw him after church. What was everyone so afraid of?

Maybe the ghosts were trying to tell him something. They whispered of secrets in Aubrey's Landing.

Celeste set her lime gelatin salad on the long table filled with covered dishes. She'd hesitated to bring the pineapple and mini-marshmallow-filled concoction after her experience in the hospital cafeteria, but it was Mia's favorite. She glanced nervously around the room, hoping not to see a certain raven-haired man with sultry eyes and a sexy smile.

No sign of him yet. She let out a whoosh of breath. "Come on, sweetie," she said, taking Mia's hand. "I see Patti and Rowena over there."

Damn him, she thought as she made her way across the crowded fellowship hall, for coming back to Aubrey's Landing to disrupt her life. And for still having the power to throw her into an emotional tailspin.

She didn't usually cuss this close to the church but *darn* didn't pack the emotional wallop she needed. Quickly, she crossed herself, the gesture automatic. She'd seen Rosa do it a million times growing up, as protection against evil thoughts or people.

Patti and Rowena sat at the table farthest from the kitchen, their heads bent over a checkerboard. Through the tall windows to their left, Celeste saw several children dash across the courtyard to the preschool play area. On Sundays, the preschool doubled as a nursery and Sunday school.

"Hey, you two. Must be a good game." Celeste swung her legs over the bench-style seat.

Patti gave her a welcoming smile. "Actually, we were just killing time until you got here. Rowena's dying to play dolls with Mia."

The little girls had been on the phone that afternoon, planning what they'd bring to the church social. Each came with a favorite doll, a suitcase full of accessories, and lots of imagination.

"Can we go now, Mom?" Mia asked.

"Sure, honey, but only for about half an hour. Then it will be time to eat." She handed Mia the folded quilt she carried.

Celeste and Patti watched as their daughters hurried out the door, eager to immerse themselves in the world of make-believe. The girls ignored the other children, heading for the tallest cottonwood tree. They spread the faded patchwork quilt underneath and began unpacking their doll clothes, chattering all the while.

Celeste sighed. "Sometimes I wish they were a little more sociable."

"All children are different. Our girls had to deal with loss at a young age."

Celeste noticed her normally bubbly friend looked troubled. "Is Rowena's dad still vying for the title of World's Biggest Jerk?"

Patti nodded. "He promised he'd come and see her this weekend. It's Sunday evening and he hasn't even called. It just breaks my heart to see Rowena hurt." Patti's blue eyes misted over as she watched the girls play.

Celeste reached across the table and squeezed her friend's hand. "I'm grateful they have each other."

Patti returned the pressure. "Me too." She dug a tissue out of her purse and dabbed at her eyes. "Want to finish the game? Rowena was winning."

Celeste grinned. "Sure."

"How are you feeling?" Patti asked. "Mia said you had a headache." She moved a red checker diagonally across the center of the board.

"It was a doozy." Celeste inched a black piece forward. "I'm still a little shaky, but the pain's gone."

Patti scrutinized her over the game board. "You do look pale. Maybe you should have stayed home."

The thought had crossed her mind. The last thing she wanted was to run into Ray again, but she couldn't crawl into a hole for however long he intended to stay. She was determined to show him she was completely unaffected by his presence in Aubrey's Landing.

Besides, she didn't want to disappoint the girls. She opened her mouth to say so, when she noticed Patti staring across the room.

He stood just inside the door, weight slightly forward, over the balls of his feet. He still had a boxer's stance, conveying quickness and power. His black jeans and cream polo shirt were unexceptional, or would have been on any other man. On Ray Fontana, they looked good enough to draw every pair of female eyes in the room.

And damn him for being so sexy, Celeste added.

"Look who's here," Patti said.

Celeste quickly turned away, her resolve evaporating. "Did he see us?" she whispered. She wasn't ready for this. Maybe she could still take Mia and go home.

Patti smiled and waved. "He just waved at me. He's taking a dish to the buffet table. What gives with you two anyway?"

"It's a long story." She remained hunched stiffly over the checkerboard, her back to Ray, hoping he'd choose to sit somewhere else. Anywhere but with her. "What's he doing now?"

Patti peered through the milling crowd. "He's setting down his dish. Now he's talking to Reverend Micah." She paused, her voice concerned. "Are you sure you're okay?"

No, Celeste wanted to scream, *I'm not okay.* Instead, she took a deep breath and willed herself to relax. "Of course. I just wasn't looking forward to meeting Ray again. We had a relationship years ago that ended badly. I haven't seen him since."

The dinner bell brought a crew of warm, flushed children running through the door. Under the cottonwood tree, Mia and Rowena folded their blanket and gathered doll clothes.

"Heads up," Patti said in a low voice. "Here he comes."

Okay, calm, cool, and collected, Celeste reminded herself. The guys at the hospital had dubbed her the Ice Princess. They hadn't even begun to see chilly yet.

"Hello, ladies. May I join you for dinner?"

Celeste turned a glance on him that would have frozen another man's blood. Ray smiled, unflinching. His brown eyes caressed her, probing the secrets of her heart. She feared if she returned his gaze much longer, Ray would know all. Dear God, why did this man have such power over her?

"Mr. Fontana!" Rowena's delighted squeal broke the spell. The little girls trooped through the door, arms full of dolls and their accessories. "Are you gonna eat with us?"

"I'd like to, if it's all right with your moms."

Patti looked uncomfortable but remained silent. Celeste glanced at Mia, who was watching her with a mixture of awe and curiosity. For Mia's sake, she had to be strong.

"Of course," she said. "You're welcome to join us."

"Goody!" Rowena clapped her hands. Mia hung back, but looked pleased. Children were drawn by Ray's energy and magnetism. Just as she had been.

"Would you ladies like to accompany me to the banquet?" He bowed and held out an arm. "Lady Rowena?"

Rowena giggled, then dipped and pulled out the sides of her shorts in a curtsey.

"And the fair Mia?" Ray extended his other arm.

Mia hesitated for a moment, glancing from Rowena to Ray and back again. It was too good to pass up. With a tiny smile, she tucked her hand in the crook of Ray's arm.

"Well." Patti shook her head in amazement as the threesome walked to the buffet table. "I've never seen them warm up to someone so fast."

Celeste couldn't keep the note of bitterness from her voice. "Oh, he can be charming, all right. As long as there's no commitment involved."

Chapter Three

*F*latter than a tortilla. Celeste stared in dismay at her right rear tire. She knew her tires were getting threadbare but had hoped to squeeze a few more miles out of them. On her salary, new tires were a necessity she couldn't quite afford.

A deep voice sounded behind her. "Looks like you could use a lift."

Ray, holding what was left of a dish of beanie weenies, stood less than three feet away. Where had he come from anyway? She'd helped with the cleanup after dinner, partly to avoid Ray's company. He should have gone home long ago.

Celeste cast around for another source of help. The parking lot was almost empty now. She could

go back into the fellowship hall and look for
Micah . . .

"Mommy, I'm tired."

Mia leaned heavily against her mother's side,
looking up with sleepy eyes. Poor little thing, she
had a busy evening and it was past her bedtime. For
Mia's sake, she'd keep up a pretense of civility. A
few more minutes of Ray's company wouldn't kill
her. With any luck, she'd be able to avoid him for
the rest of his stay.

She stiffened her spine and turned to face him.
"If it's not too much trouble. We don't live far."

"No trouble at all."

In the dimly lit parking lot, Celeste thought she
saw a flicker of triumph in Ray's eyes. He led the
way to a mid-size sedan parked under a street light.

"The lot was full when I arrived so I parked on
the street." He unlocked the driver's side door, then
reached inside and flipped up the lock in back.
"You look sleepy, princess. Want to get comfy in
the backseat?"

Mia nodded. Ray buckled her into the car,
tucked a soft pillow under her head and covered her
with the patchwork quilt. Mia rewarded him with a
smile before closing her eyes.

Celeste hovered close by, juggling the doll and
suitcase, her purse and a half-eaten dish of lime
gelatin. An ugly suspicion nibbled at her consciousness. Could it have been a coincidence that

Ray showed up just as she left the hall and discovered the flat tire? And what about the pillow in his backseat? It all seemed a little too convenient. "Are you always so well prepared?" she asked.

"I always carry a pillow when I travel, if that's what you mean. Hotel pillows feel like sacks of cement." He rounded the car with Celeste at his heels, stopping to deposit his dish of beanie weenies in the trunk.

"Why didn't you unlock the doors with the master switch?" All new cars had one. Surely, Ray must be aware of that fact.

Ray reached the passenger door, inserted the key and pulled it open. "My mother taught me that a gentleman always opens the door for a lady. Here, let me help you with that." He took the doll and suitcase from her.

A dozen scathing remarks popped into her head, but Celeste pressed her lips together and climbed into the car. She set the dish on the seat between them, then smoothed her walking shorts to cover as much of her legs as possible. After all, she *was* a lady, even if Ray Fontana was no gentleman.

Ray chuckled, as if he had guessed her thoughts. He shut her door and walked around the rear of the vehicle. Moments later he slid behind the wheel. "Where to?" he asked.

"We live near Copper Canyon Estates. In Nilson Heights. Do you remember how to get there?"

"Sure. It's the nicest neighborhood in town." He turned on his headlights and pulled out onto the deserted street.

"I said we live *near* Copper Canyon Estates, not in it. Dad donated the adjacent forty acres to the city and they built affordable houses for working people. Like me." It galled her for Ray to think she'd been handed the world on a silver platter. She worked hard to get where she was, and didn't appreciate being cast in the role of a spoiled little rich girl. "Turn left at the next corner, on Mountain View."

Ray glanced in her direction. Only the rhythmic click-click of his turn signal broke the silence.

"It's right here."

They pulled in front of a neat, one-story stucco. A long covered porch shaded its west-facing front. Celeste's house looked pretty much like the others on her street, with the exception of the place next door. Jagged glass jutted from its window frames and the screen door hung at a crazy angle. Weeds and windblown trash decorated the front yard, along with a Hometown Realty sign.

"Thank you for the ride." Celeste unlatched her seat belt and reached for the door handle.

"Wait."

The word hung in the air between them. Reluctantly, she released the handle.

"I didn't mean to offend you. I don't know much about your life, except that you have a beautiful little girl. I'd like to talk with you for a minute. There are some things I need to explain."

He made no attempt to touch her. If he had, she'd have bolted. But his eyes burned into her. Ray had the darkest eyes she'd ever seen, almost black. *It must be his Native American heritage.* The thought drifted through her brain, as Ray's gaze held her captive.

Okay, enough of this nonsense. She gathered her purse with her right hand, carefully balancing the plastic-wrapped dish of gelatin with her left. She didn't intend to embarrass herself in front of Ray again. One baptism by gelatin was enough for this lifetime.

"It's late, Ray. I have work in the morning and Mia has school. Besides, anything you had to say should have been said eight years ago." She opened the door, flooding the interior of the car with light. Mia whimpered and pulled the blanket over her face.

"Wait," he said again. "Please."

Celeste hesitated. Maybe she wasn't being fair. Maybe if she listened to his explanation, he'd go away and leave her alone. She shut the door, but didn't look at him. "Okay, but make it quick. I have a busy day tomorrow."

Her ungracious reply made Celeste even more uncomfortable. She was reminded of the story Rosa told about a woman who had nothing but evil things to say. Finally, a powerful *bruja,* a witch, grew tired of the woman's rudeness and cast a spell on her. Thereafter, scorpions, snakes, and lizards fell out of the unfortunate woman's mouth whenever she opened it.

All right, she thought. It's the best I can do. If it took a few snakes and lizards to keep Ray Fontana at a distance, then so be it. She had to protect herself and Mia.

Through the front windshield, bright pinpoints of light gleamed in the black velvet sky. Ray hesitated so long before speaking that she sneaked a glance in his direction. His face was partially in shadow but she could make out the high cheekbone, the flat plane of his cheek, and a strong angular jaw. Long ago, she'd memorized that face, with her lips and fingertips.

"I came to your house the day before Labor Day, eight years ago. Your father said you'd gone back to school in Phoenix." He continued to stare straight ahead.

Celeste felt her stomach twist. "That's not true! Rosa and I went to Phoenix, but only to shop. I was home the next day, waiting for you."

Ray nodded in the semi-darkness. "I figured as much. Your father would have said anything to keep us apart. Like a lot of people in this town, he figured I was just like my old man. A bad seed." His voice sounded harsh, brittle.

Despite herself, Celeste felt the old tenderness

seep into her heart. What must it have been like to grow up in Aubrey's Landing as the son of Al Fontana? No wonder Ray always felt he had to be tougher, smarter, faster than anyone.

"He told me I couldn't offer you the kind of life you deserved. He said I might be a hero in some people's eyes but folks around here hadn't forgotten the fights, the juvenile record, the years I spent at Boys Ranch. He said you'd have to live with gossip and stares for the rest of your life, because wherever I went my past would follow."

"Why did you believe him, Ray?" Celeste couldn't keep the anguish from her voice. She gripped the Pyrex dish so tight her hands ached. "You knew I loved you."

Ray tilted his face in her direction. His tone was soft, the words gentle. "Yes, you loved me, with a sweetness and honesty I haven't found since. Your father convinced me I was doing you a favor. He told me I wouldn't be able to leave if I saw you again, and I knew he was right. So I packed up that night, and got the hell out of Aubrey's Landing."

Suddenly, Celeste felt flooded with anger. A lifetime of anger. It surged through her bloodstream, threatening to drown her. She slammed the gelatin dish down on her lap. "I am so sick of men deciding what's best for me. Did it ever occur to either of you to ask what *I* wanted?"

Ray blinked at her in surprise. "I guess not."

As quickly as it had come, the flood receded. Absurdly, she felt like giggling. "No, I guess it wouldn't. Well, Ray, I appreciate the explanation. I need to get Mia to bed now." She opened the car door and stepped out into the night.

Within seconds, Ray jumped out, too. "Let me carry Mia in for you. There's no sense in waking her. You get her doll and suitcase. They're in the trunk."

She opened her mouth to protest but he already had the back door open and was bundling Mia into his arms. The child snuggled against his chest.

He was quick on his feet, Celeste thought. Always had been. She'd been trying all night to avoid him, and now he'd maneuvered his way into her home. She shook her head as she followed him up the sidewalk to her front porch. What did the man want from her?

Celeste walked around him, being careful not to touch any part of his body with any part of hers. She inserted the key into the door, then pushed it open, standing aside so he could pass. Quite a feat while juggling four items. "Mia's room is the first door on your left."

She dumped everything on the kitchen table, then tiptoed after him down the hall. Mia hardly stirred as Ray placed her on the twin bed. He stood for a moment looking down at her. "Do you want to put her pajamas on?" he whispered.

"She can sleep in her clothes tonight," Celeste answered from the doorway.

Carefully, he pulled off Mia's tennis shoes, then tucked the sheet and coverlet under her chin. Celeste lingered, watching. He seemed so gentle and loving with Mia. For a moment, she felt a pang of conscience. Was she wrong to keep Mia's parentage a secret?

Maybe, but she'd rather live with that sin on her conscience than risk hurting her daughter. Ray might be Mia's biological father, but he'd left them long ago. Even now, he was only visiting for a short while. She wouldn't, couldn't, rearrange their lives to include him.

What if Ray turned out to be like Rowena's father? Celeste suppressed a shudder. No, she'd stick with her plan to raise Mia alone. Eventually, she'd tell Mia about her father, when she was old enough to understand. Right now, her daughter needed love and stability, not another big upset. She'd already been through too much in her short life.

Ray walked out of the room, his footsteps barely audible on the carpeted floor. Celeste closed Mia's door, then followed him down the hall. She couldn't help admiring Ray's fluid, catlike walk. He moved with such grace and agility, so sure of himself. She'd always envied his self-confidence.

He wasn't a big man, standing only two inches taller than her. Oh, but the vitality he packed into that body. She watched, hypnotized by the smooth synchronization of muscular thighs, narrow hips, and perfectly proportioned shoulders. If Ray hadn't taken up boat racing, he could have been a dancer.

Her thoughts were interrupted as Ray abruptly stopped at the entrance to the living room. She skidded to a halt, missing a rear-end collision by millimeters. Quickly, she hopped back, praying he hadn't noticed.

What was he doing, anyway? Hadn't she made it clear the evening was over? There wasn't enough room to navigate around him in the narrow hallway. At least, not without touching him, and that was the last thing she wanted to do. She pushed her hair back from her forehead in an impatient gesture and mentally willed him to move.

"Your home is lovely. You have a nice touch. With decorating, I mean." He turned and gave her a disarming smile, his eyes seeking hers.

Trapped. Celeste experienced a moment of panic. She felt like a rabbit caught in the merciless gaze of a mountain lion. "Thank you. It's probably a little feminine for a man's taste but Mia and I like it. I mean, it's home."

Dear God, what was she babbling about? Ray's aura, his masculine essence filled the narrow hallway. His hooded eyes glittered in the darkness and she could have sworn she smelled the sweet scent of pine smoke.

The hallway, so ordinary in the daylight, became an intimate enclave. She took a step backward, then another. Ray matched her step for step. *The predator stalking his prey.*

Say something, she thought, *anything.* "I haven't done much with the yard yet. It needs to be landscaped and fenced. I'm afraid I just haven't had the time."

She'd backed herself into a corner now. The back of her legs touched a narrow bookcase and she felt the picture of Great-Grandfather and Great-Grandmother Johansen press against her rear. Ray stood directly in front of her, cutting off any escape.

"I can help you, Celeste, if you'll let me. I've always been good with my hands." As if to prove his statement, he raised one hand and let the fingers trail down her cheek.

She watched him, transfixed. She felt paralyzed, whether by fear or fascination, she wasn't sure. She only knew she was powerless to stop him. His fingertips awakened every nerve-ending in her body. She ached and trembled for his touch. As his hand slid behind her neck, she closed her eyes and awaited the pressure of his lips.

His mouth found hers. The kiss was warm and seductive. She tilted her head back to give him better access and a small moan escaped her lips. She twined the fingers of her left hand through his thick hair and hung on for dear life.

There it was again. The smell of pine smoke, with a hint of earthy musk. She hadn't imagined it. Ray placed his hand in the small of her back, pulling her against his hard chest as he deepened the kiss.

A tantalizing warmth spread throughout her body. It reminded her of Rosa's mole sauce, made of rich, dark chocolate and chile. Sweet and yet deliciously spicy. She reached back with her right hand, groping for support.

A loud crash awoke her from the trance. Her eyes flew open and fixed in terror on Ray. *Santos!* What was she thinking? What was she doing?

Panicked, she backed away from him and straight into the bookcase. The picture of Great-Grandfather and Great-Grandmother Johansen teetered precariously. Celeste reached down to steady it. When she looked up, Ray was watching her. She saw passion in his eyes but also a disconcerting sureness. She'd responded to him like a beggar at a banquet. And he knew it.

She glanced at the picture lying on the linoleum floor. She should have carpeted the hallway when they moved in, but there were so many expenses and so little money. Dr. Leander Nilson looked up at her accusingly, shards of broken glass littering his white hospital jacket. It was her father's favorite photograph, taken when he was chief of staff at Aubrey's Landing Medical Center.

Thank goodness they hadn't awakened Mia. Her face burned as she pictured her daughter wandering into the hallway and finding her in Ray's embrace. Definitely *not* the kind of example she wanted to set.

She pulled the tatters of her dignity around her. "I really must ask you to leave."

"Let me help you clean up first." Ray stooped to pick up the picture.

"No!" The word came out a bit too forcefully but she didn't care. Right now, she just wanted to get Ray out the door. She hurried into the living room, eager to escape the scene of her humiliation.

Light, that was what she needed. Lots of light. Glaring light to let Ray know she was in no mood for his romantic advances. She switched on the overhead lights in the living room and the chandelier in the dining room.

Would it be too obvious to turn on the living room lamps, too? she wondered. Why not? At this point, she had nothing to lose. She was twisting the knob on a lamp when Ray spoke.

"I tried to contact you in Phoenix."

It took a minute for his words to penetrate the shame and confusion that filled her brain. She turned and stared at him dumbly. "In Phoenix?" she repeated.

"Yeah, at that private college. My letters weren't answered and when I called, you were never in. After a couple of months the matron, or warden, told me you'd left school to get married."

Celeste stood in the middle of the room, bathed in blessed, blazing, protective light. She felt a little stronger now, in the familiar world of her living room. "She was the dorm mother."

"More like a prison guard, if you ask me. Anyway, shortly afterward I received all my letters back, unopened. I knew we'd both been lied to, but I figured it was too late to do anything about it."

Ray crossed to where she stood and took one of her hands in his. His voice became low and intimate, like the purr of a big cat. "I never stopped thinking about you."

Celeste jerked her hand back. He was coming on to her again! With all the lights on! The man had absolutely no scruples.

"Just what do you want from me, Ray? My forgiveness? Fine, I forgive you for running out on me without a word. I forgive you for breaking my heart. You are absolved of all guilt. Now, will you please leave?" She massaged her temples with trembling fingers.

Still, he stood there. She didn't know what else to do, short of shoving him out the door, or calling the police. Wouldn't that be a pretty scene for Mia to wake up to?

He didn't seem dangerous, merely stubborn.

She'd just have to play this game out. Warily, she waited for his next move.

Ray shifted his weight slightly forward, unconsciously assuming a fighter's stance. Although his hands hung loosely at his sides, Celeste sensed the adrenaline pulsing through his body. His voice was deceptively soft. "I appreciate your forgiveness. Really, I do. But it's not enough. I want a second chance."

She stared at him in disbelief, opened her mouth and then closed it again. Could he be joking? No, his striking features were as serious as those of Great-Grandfather Johansen in the antique photograph. She'd thought nothing Ray could say or do would shock her, not after this evening. Wrong, again.

Just how could she answer a statement like that? How could she convince him, once and for all time, that a relationship between them could never, ever work? So many reasons occurred to her, she didn't know where to begin.

Cool, calm, and collected. If ever there was a time for the Ice Princess to make an appearance, it was now. Celeste drew herself up to her full five foot eight inches and marched regally to the door. She held it open, looking him squarely in the eye.

"I'm sorry if I gave you the wrong impression. What happened between us was long ago, and best forgotten. Let me be perfectly clear. I have a busy life and I don't have the time or the interest in renewing our acquaintance. Good night, Ray."

Not even Ray Fontana could ignore that dismissal. He brushed against her ever so slightly as he passed through the door. Unfair, unnecessary, and definitely threatening to her icy facade. The man played dirty.

"Good night, angel," he murmured.

Celeste shut and locked the door. Then she pressed her back against the cool wood and slid slowly to the floor.

Ray grinned at his reflection in the mirror. The jagged scar over his left eye was almost invisible now, except when he was angry or excited. Tonight, it stood out like a bolt of lightning.

He hadn't felt this alive in years. The corporate takeovers, the humble obeisance of his former business rivals, even the attention of the most beautiful women in Miami—none of it came close to the thrill he'd experienced in Celeste's hallway.

She tried to put him in his place but it was too late. He'd seen the warm, sensuous, exciting woman beneath that frigid exterior, and he knew he had the power to awaken her.

"It's just a matter of time, angel."

He grabbed a towel and dried his face. He'd shower in the morning and then head over to Gus' shop.

Or maybe he'd do a little detective work first.

Delve into the mysteries of Aubrey's Landing. Ray pulled down the spread, stripped off his shorts and threw himself down on the cool sheets.

Yeah, tomorrow would be a good day to unearth a few secrets. And he knew just where to start.

Chapter Four

Ray opened the front door to Gustav's Bait, Boat, and Sports Emporium, locally known as The Bait Shop. Marine accessories, bright orange life jackets, outboard oil, marine resin, props, anchors, and assorted hardware filled the shelves. Along the back wall, all manner of fishing tackle jostled against the live bait tank.

Only Gus could make order of this chaos, and Gus was home recuperating from a heart attack. Ray sincerely hoped the old man had put price tags on all this junk. He hadn't bought a can of outboard oil or a fishing pole within recent memory, and didn't have a clue what to charge for them. He picked up a can, turning it around to view all sides. Nothing.

With a sigh, he pulled a notepad from his back pocket. *Look for price list,* he wrote. Now to check out the other half of the business.

He took a sharp right, past the long counter that held the cash register, stopping for just a moment to inspect the exotic collection of fishing lures and flies displayed in the glass case. Gus had given him a set of keys but he didn't need them. The door between the shop and garage was wide open. He frowned and got out his notepad. *Talk to Gus about security.*

Gus had already been robbed once. That violent night brought the two of them together, forever altering Ray's destiny. Everyone credited him with saving Gus' life but it hadn't really been a conscious decision on his part. In fact, he'd been just as surprised by his own actions as he had by those of his so-called friend, Dante Rodriquez.

They'd come to the store late at night and jimmied open the back window of the garage. Then, as now, the door between the garage and store was unlocked.

Clean out the cash register and run. That was the plan. They hadn't counted on Gus working late in the basement of the garage. He caught them red-handed.

Ray could still see the look of shock on the old man's face when the bullet hit him. He'd clutched his chest and staggered back against the doorway, blood seeping between his fingers. Ray looked in horror at his friend. Dante stood with his feet apart, knees bent, holding the gun with both hands.

Dante grabbed the money and ran into the garage. "Let's get out of here," he yelled.

Ray panicked and started to follow. He got as far as the door when Gus called out, his voice coarse with pain. "Help me. Please."

In that split second, Ray made a choice that would change his life. He turned, walked back into the store and called 911.

The police and ambulance arrived at about the same time. The officers handcuffed Ray while paramedics lifted Gus onto a stretcher. The old man had lost a lot of blood and looked close to death. As he passed Ray on the way to the ambulance, Gus spoke, his voice a low rasp. "I won't forget this."

And he hadn't. Ray had saved Gus' life once, more as a gut reaction than out of any goodness or nobility. Gus had been looking out for him ever since.

He turned on the light and rolled up the garage door. Only one boat sat inside, waiting to be repaired. The motor overhaul Gus had mentioned. He walked over and peered at the engine.

"You must be Al Fontana's boy."

Instantly the hairs at the back of Ray's neck stood up. He'd heard those words before and they were never meant as a compliment. He shot a murderous look over his shoulder and saw a rotund senior citizen in overalls and tennis shoes, clutching a cigar.

The old man backed up a step, holding up both hands. "Hey, take it easy, fella. I didn't mean any harm. I knew your daddy years ago. He was the best shade tree mechanic in the county and a damn fine carpenter too."

"That was before my time," Ray said. "When I knew him, all he did was drink." He walked over and extended a hand. "My name's Ray."

The man grinned and a network of furrows spread across his face. He slipped the cigar into the front pocket of his overalls and pumped Ray's hand. "Clarence Rogers. Gus lets me hang around here. It's sort of my home away from home." He pointed to an ugly brown recliner, flanked by a couple of hard-backed chairs, a soda pop machine and a water cooler. The corkboard overhead read: *Senior Citizen Day Care Center.*

Ray liked the amiable old character. "That's fine with me, but don't expect to loaf all day. With Gus out of commission, I'm going to need help running this place."

Clarence stood a little straighter and threw out his chest. "Why, I'd be proud to help."

"Good. Then maybe you could keep an eye on the store while I tackle this engine." How did Gus manage both businesses at once? he wondered. Especially at his age.

Clarence gave him a jaunty salute, then shuffled through the doorway.

Was he ever going to smoke that cigar? Or did he just carry it around? Ray shook his head. Too many questions. Rolling up his sleeves, he turned his attention to the engine. It had been a long time since he'd gotten his hands dirty.

Tear it down, bore it, sleeve it and put rings in. Gus' words echoed through the years. Maybe working on boat motors was something you never forgot, like riding a bicycle. He sure hoped so.

He pulled the notepad from his pocket one last time. *Hire help,* he wrote. And then, a single word: *secrets.*

The phone rang insistently as Celeste approached her office on Friday morning. Friday the thirteenth. How she dreaded these days. As a responsible working mother, she couldn't stay in bed with the covers over her head. That wouldn't set a good example for Mia, and more than anything, she wanted to set a good example for Mia.

Act as if, she told herself. As if you're not frightened, as if you're not superstitious, as if you have all the answers. Hah! As if.

Grasping her sack lunch between her teeth, Celeste balanced her purse and a stack of paperwork while she unlocked the door.

"Hold your horses," she muttered around the

sack. She shoved the door open with her knee and ran for the phone, leaving a trail of papers fluttering to the carpet behind her. "Herrow?" she mumbled around her lunch.

There was a pause on the other end of the line. "Celeste? Is that you?"

Celeste automatically stood a little straighter. She pulled the paper bag out of her mouth and suppressed a sigh. The day was not beginning well. "Yes, Father, it's me."

"I hear Ray Fontana's back in town."

He came right to the point. You had to give him that. "I saw him in church on Sunday."

"And at the church social Sunday night."

For a wild, paranoid moment, Celeste wondered if her father knew Ray had given her a ride home and kissed her in the hallway. She held the phone away from her mouth, took a deep breath and let it out slowly. *Calm down,* she told herself. Dr. Nilson's spies weren't *that* good.

"It's a free country." As soon as the words were out of her mouth, she regretted them. Her father still had the power to turn her into a sullen twelve-year-old.

Dr. Nilson's voice took on the cold, distant tone he used when she behaved badly as a child. "Yes, I'm aware of that, Celeste."

Celeste closed her eyes and pressed the phone to her forehead. Although she saw her father every evening, she'd avoided any mention of Ray's return. Her father hated Ray. Always had, always would. She felt sure her father was convinced he'd done the right thing by trying to protect her from Ray. When had he ever been wrong?

The past was past. There was no point in stirring that pot of *menudo*, tripe stew. "Sorry, Father. It's been a difficult week."

"I understand." His voice let her know he did not understand, nor did he appreciate her flippant attitude. "If he should try to contact you or bother you in any way . . ."

Celeste hurried to appease him. "Don't worry. He's only going to be here for a short time. I'm sure I won't run into him again." At least, not if I can help it, she thought.

She said good-bye and began picking up papers. The stroke that had made her father a semi-invalid certainly hadn't robbed him of his forceful character. If anything, he'd become even more domineering and inflexible. She'd learned to avoid confrontations with him. What good did it do to argue? Despite her father's faults, she still loved him.

"Hey, beautiful. Need some help?"

From her crouched position on the floor, Celeste looked up into the too-pretty face of Dr. Giorgio Bandini, also known as Gorgeous George. Immediately, a wave of aftershave assaulted her nostrils. An oft-repeated joke at the hospital claimed the anesthesiologist didn't need to drug his patients. He just splashed on a little more cologne.

Celeste scrambled to her feet, pasting on a friendly smile. "Dr. Bandini. What a nice surprise." Actually, she wasn't surprised at all. Dr. Bandini had been like a gnat buzzing around her head since he'd arrived at the hospital six months ago. Her insistence that she didn't date only seemed to make him buzz harder.

The doctor's dark, limpid gaze traveled slowly down her body and back up again. "I came to invite you to breakfast. The first surgery isn't scheduled until ten o'clock, so I find myself with a little time to kill."

Celeste had to restrain herself from crossing her arms over her chest. The man made her feel undressed. "I'm sorry, Dr. Bandini. I really am much too busy." She gestured toward the neat stacks of papers on her desk.

Dr. Bandini waggled his finger at her. "Always busy. I think you are too busy for your own good. You should learn to relax, have a little fun."

Celeste walked to the door and held it open. "Thank you, Doctor. I'll consider your advice."

What next? Celeste thought as she shut the door behind him. Bad luck came in threes and she'd had two unpleasant encounters before she had a chance to set down her purse.

Gorgeous George she could handle. She tolerated the man because he was an excellent anesthesiologist, despite having an ego the size of three western states. Cool professionalism kept the doctor at arm's length. Her father, however, was another story. An argument with him still rattled her to the core.

Celeste crossed gingerly to her desk, expecting the third curse to befall her at any moment. She pulled the religious medallion from its hiding place under her blouse and rubbed it between her fingers. Rosa had given her the medallion years ago, when Celeste was a little girl. She'd worn it ever since.

Leaving the necklace outside her blouse, Celeste flipped through papers. Discharge planning forms, a report of domestic violence, transfers to alcohol and drug rehabilitation centers, and her notes from counseling two young women who showed up in the emergency room to have their babies.

Of all the human tragedies she witnessed in the hospital, the young mothers affected her the most. Alone and frightened, they often were barely old enough to take care of themselves, much less their babies. Although Celeste did her best to help the young women take advantage of the services available, they were largely on their own. She knew it and so did they.

She'd attended a discouraging meeting of the Obstetrics Center committee the previous evening in the hospital conference room. Even with their hard work and the support of many in the community, it looked as though the new OB Center was still a distant dream. They just didn't have the financing.

Someday . . . Celeste's thought was interrupted by the ringing phone. She looked at it as if it were a rattlesnake, poised to strike. The third piece of bad luck. She could feel it in her bones. Gripping the medallion in one hand, she picked up the receiver.

"Social Services."

"Walker? We need you in the emergency room."

She recognized the gravelly voice immediately. Marge Wilmer, the Assistant Director of Nursing, smoked two packs a day and could put the most arrogant doctor in his place with a few well-chosen words. Marge's rough exterior couldn't conceal her marshmallow center. She was always the first to open her heart and pocketbook to anyone in need.

"I'm on my way."

Bad luck temporarily forgotten, Celeste hurried out the door and down the hall, her heels clicking against the gleaming tile floors. A summons to the ER was serious, but not uncommon. Although her title proclaimed her the head of social services, in truth, she was the only social worker at the hundred-bed hospital. Whenever a patient or family member needed counseling, crisis intervention, a referral, transfer to another facility, or just a shoulder to cry on, the staff called Celeste.

Had there been an accident? she wondered. Or maybe another woman in labor? She turned the last corner and pushed open the double doors leading to the ER hallway. Karon, a pretty redheaded emergency medical technician, waited for her just outside the locked doors of the emergency room.

"Hi, Karon. What's up?" she asked.

"Marge wants you to meet her at the swamp." Karon referred to the employee smoking area outside the cafeteria.

That seemed a little odd. Maybe Marge wanted to consult with her about a patient, away from prying eyes and ears. Celeste walked outside and took a right. Just beyond the ambulance entrance to the emergency room, she saw the bluish haze of cigarette smoke rising from the swamp.

A crowd of hospital workers seemed to be examining something on the ground. Celeste was thirty feet away when Marge hailed her.

"Hey, Walker. We've got a problem here."

An ex-Army nurse, Marge had never been able to break the habit of calling her coworkers by their last names. Celeste frequently had the urge to salute when Marge addressed her. So far, she'd managed to resist the impulse.

"Tell me about it." As she sat down next to the gray-haired veteran a single, heartbreaking howl rent the air. The trauma-hardened hospital workers gave a collective chorus of "Ohhhhh." They shifted slightly and Celeste glimpsed the object of their sympathy.

A scruffy, medium-sized tan dog lay with his head on his paws. His big, sorrowful brown eyes scanned the crowd. Bowls of food and water sat untouched beside him. He looked like a terrier but with that voice, there had to be hound in the gene pool.

Marge spoke in a low, confidential tone. "Pooch's owner was living in a hotel room, one of those rent-by-the-week places. He had a heart attack. When the ambulance showed up, the old guy wouldn't go without his dog, so the EMTs brought Pooch along. That's just between the two of us." She paused to take a drag on her cigarette. "The old guy didn't make it."

It took a minute for Celeste to grasp why Marge had called her. "You want me to find a home for Pooch?" she asked. She'd had some strange requests during her two years at the medical center, but this was first time she'd been asked to do crisis intervention for a dog.

"You've got a kid, don't you? Why don't you take him?"

Celeste noticed a suspicious moistness in Marge's steely blue eyes. Some tough character. "Sorry, Marge. I'd like to help but we're away from home so much, it wouldn't be fair to Pooch. Mia stays with her Grandma Rosa until I get off work, which is frequently at six or seven o'clock. How about you?"

"I already have two dogs and three cats. If I bring

home any more strays, my roommates will shoot me. That's no joke. They're all combat veterans."

"What about the Greek chorus over there?" Celeste gestured toward the group of hospital workers gathered around Pooch.

Marge ticked the excuses off on her fingers. "Can't have pets. Kid's afraid of dogs. Husband's allergic to dogs. Oh, and a vicious cockatiel."

"Well, we certainly can't place Pooch with a vicious cockatiel. Come here, boy." Celeste wiggled her fingers at the dog.

Pooch rolled his eyes in her direction, wagged his tail a couple of times but didn't get up.

"I'll take the dog."

Strike three. She should have known. All week she'd eaten lunch in her office to avoid running into Ray. The one time she ventured into the cafeteria, who should be waiting for her? Dudley Do-Right.

She turned and faced her tormenter. He lounged in the doorway, looking like a near occasion of sin in his tight jeans and form-fitting T-shirt. "You can't have him," she said.

Out of the corner of her eye, Celeste saw Marge looking at her like she'd developed a strange and unsightly rash. "I mean you won't be here long enough. You are leaving town aren't you?"

A smile twisted the corners of Ray's mouth. Ignoring the curious glances of the employees, he spoke to Celeste as if they were alone on the patio.

"Actually, no. I bought a house in Aubrey's Landing and I plan to live here. Indefinitely."

A chill raced up her spine. It couldn't be true. "You bought a house?" she repeated.

Ray nodded. "A fixer-upper. It needs a lot of work but it's in a great neighborhood. Nilson Heights. You may have heard of it."

A vision of the house next door flashed in her head. The previous owners had trashed the place, then walked away from the mortgage. She couldn't imagine having worse neighbors. Unless . . ."

"You didn't."

"Yeah, I did." Ray walked over and squatted beside the dog. He held out his hand so Pooch could sniff it, then scratched behind the dog's ears. "Come on, old fellow."

In a quick, graceful movement, Ray rose. Muscles rippled, tendons flexed, the man was poetry in motion. He flashed her a sardonic grin and a half salute. "Be seeing you, neighbor."

Pooch trotted obediently after him.

"I'd watch myself around that man, Walker. He has a dangerous look about him."

Celeste chose to ignore the teasing note in Marge's voice. The woman had no idea how dangerous Ray really was. "You're telling me," she muttered.

It hit her as soon as she opened the door. That smell could only be *sopa de albóndigas.* How did

Rosa know she needed comfort food at the end of this day? She'd go upstairs and say good night to her father later. Right now, she craved the warmth and love in Rosa's kitchen.

"Mama!" Mia ran up and gave her a big hug. "Grandma Rosa's teaching me to make *buñuelos!*"

"I can see that." Celeste wiped a streak of flour from her daughter's cheek. "Did Rosa teach you to make meatball soup too?"

Mia looked disappointed. "No, she cooked that before I came home."

"I'll teach you to make soup, little one, and tacos, enchiladas, tamales—just like I taught your mother." Rosa stood at the sink, up to her elbows in soapy water. Her braided salt-and-pepper hair formed a crown on top of her head. Next to her, twelve round, thin *buñuelos,* separated by layers of wax paper, waited to be dunked in boiling oil. Served hot, golden and drizzled with honey, Rosa's *buñuelos* were the closest thing to sweet perfection this side of heaven.

Celeste crossed to the sink to wash her hands. "How's Father?"

"What is the word you use? When Mia is very hungry or tired?" Rosa's brow furrowed.

"Cranky?"

Rosa nodded vigorously. "That's it. He was cranky today. I brought him a sandwich at noon. When I came back at one o'clock, he had not touched it. He was talking on the phone to Mr. Belgrave." She shot Celeste a meaningful glance.

Although Rosa's English wasn't perfect, Celeste knew from long experience that not much got by her *mamacita*. "Ah, the city attorney. They must have been talking about plans to redevelop downtown Aubrey's Landing." The redevelopment plans had half the town in an uproar, but Celeste couldn't help feeling grateful. Her father's involvement in the project had temporarily distracted him from the fact that Ray Fontana was back in town. Considering recent events, that was a very good thing indeed.

"I guess Sheila's with him now?"

Rosa wrung out her washcloth with a little more force than necessary. "She was an hour late again. I don't know why the doctor puts up with her."

Celeste didn't know for sure either, but she could guess. The night nurse must be providing a service valuable enough to make up for her lack of punctuality. Ever since his stroke two years ago, her father had assembled a network of spies to serve as his eyes and ears in the community. She had the feeling Shifty Sheila's real talents lay in areas far removed from patient care.

Rosa interrupted her musings. "You look tired. Did you have a hard day?"

"Un dia monstro." Celeste rolled her eyes at Mia, eliciting the hoped-for giggle. She draped an

arm around Rosa's plump shoulders and kissed her on the cheek. "Thank you," she said.

The older woman looked at her quizzically. "For what?"

"For always being there for me and Mia. And for your *sopa de albóndigas.*"

"*De nada.* You're welcome." Rosa dried her hands on a dish towel, then patted Celeste's cheek. "Sit down. Mia and I already had our dinner. I'll make the *buñuelos* while you eat."

Seated at the kitchen table with a steaming bowl of soup in front of her, Celeste felt her tense muscles begin to relax. As a child, this room had been her refuge. No matter how bad things seemed, she knew she could always count on Rosa's sympathetic presence and something good to eat.

"I want to hear about the monsters." Mia sat beside her mother at the table, her spelling workbook open in front of her.

"You know there aren't any real monsters, Mia."

Mia sighed. "I know. It's a finger of speech."

"Right." Celeste stuffed a meatball in her mouth to keep from smiling. "*Un día monstro* means 'a monstrous day.' "

"So tell me about the pretend monsters." Mia scooted her chair closer.

She might as well get it over with. Mia would find out about their new neighbor sooner or later. She could only hope to keep things as normal as possible. "I didn't run into any monsters today but I did meet a very nice dog. His name is Pooch, and he's going to live next door to us."

"Really?" Mia's eyes got big and round. Suddenly, a shadow crept over her features. "Are the people who played loud music coming back?"

Celeste hurried to reassure her. "No, sweetheart. The dog's new owner bought the house next to us."

"Is he the monster?"

From the mouths of babes. "No, honey. It's Ray Fontana."

"*Santos!* That one! If his *huevos* were any bigger, he'd trip over them."

Rosa stood with her back a pan of boiling oil, waving a spatula in the air. Celeste jumped up and took the spatula from her. "Let me finish here, Mamacita." She led Rosa to the table. "You sit down and rest."

Rosa fanned herself with a Mia's spelling workbook. "I'm sorry. Sometimes I get too excited."

Mia patted her hand. "It's okay, Grandma. Mama gets excited about Mr. Fontana too." Both women turned to look at her, but Mia seemed oblivious. "I hope he lets me play with his dog."

Chapter Five

"What have we gotten ourselves into, Pooch?"

Ray surveyed the interior of his new home. It looked like the morning after in a biker bar. Empty pizza cartons, beer cans, and fast food wrappers littered the floor. Someone had spray-painted "It's party time" over the fireplace in fluorescent orange letters. If there was an unbroken door or window in the house, he had yet to find it. No wonder the realtor had been so eager to sell.

Pooch lifted his nose skyward and howled.

"I know exactly how you feel, old fella. Stinks in here, doesn't it?" Ray walked through the living room to a small dining area. Pooch followed, sniffing at the piles of trash. As Ray turned the corner into the kitchen, the stench sent him reeling back. Pooch sneezed and shook his head.

"Whew! I think we'll tackle the kitchen later."

Ray retraced his steps to the living room. The floor plan was identical to Celeste's house. A central hallway led to two bedrooms and two baths. The smaller bedroom to the left was empty except for a few pieces of clothing scattered about. The master bedroom held an old mattress and more beer and liquor bottles. Cigarette burns scored the windowsill and dried puddles of candle wax clung to the carpet.

"The love palace," Ray commented dryly. Pooch woofed in response.

At least the fixtures still stood in the bathrooms, and under all the garbage, he guessed that the house was structurally sound. Definitely a fixer-upper.

Ray walked outside to the vintage Ford pickup with Gustaf's Bait, Boat, and Sports Emporium painted on the side. Gus had come home from the hospital on Friday. He'd insisted Ray use his pickup, saying it was good advertisement.

Just what a poor-but-honest mechanic would drive. Luckily, the boat repair business died down after Labor Day. He'd have plenty of time to work on his new house.

Now that he'd decided to stay in Aubrey's Landing, he'd have time to complete all his projects.

Ray glanced at the closed blinds on the house next door. He hadn't made a success of Native Spirit Boats by being weak-willed or particular about ethics. Whatever it took, by Christmas Celeste would be his.

Whistling a tune from *Fiddler on the Roof,* Ray pulled his work gloves and a twenty-gallon trash bag from the cab of the pickup and set to work.

The pounding of a hammer, combined with slightly off-key whistling greeted Celeste as she and Mia pulled into their driveway after work. Automatically, she scanned her memory until the tune clicked into place: "If I Were a Rich Man."

Cute, she thought, very cute.

Ray stood, tiles in hand, and waved at them from the roof of his new home. "Hi, neighbors. What do you think?" He swung his hammer in a wide arc over the house and yard.

Celeste surveyed his handiwork from her driveway. She hated to admit it, but the house looked pretty darn good. Ray had rid the yard of trash and replaced the broken windows in the front of the house. The place wouldn't win any chamber of commerce awards, but in one day he'd accomplished more than she thought possible.

She'd expected Ray to move in, although not quite so soon. That had to be the quickest escrow on record. She took a deep breath and squared her shoulders. Polite but distant, she reminded herself. Time to put her strategy into action.

"It looks very nice." She turned to Mia, who'd walked around the car to stand beside her. "Come on, honey. Time for dinner and a nice warm bath."

"But I want to pet Pooch," Mia protested. The tan dog lay on a rug on the long front porch, watching them.

"I don't know, Mia."

"Please, Mom. You said he was a nice dog."

Celeste couldn't resist the pleading look on Mia's face. "Okay, but just for a minute."

As they approached, Pooch thumped his tail against the wooden floorboards. The porch was one of the nicest features of these little tract homes. Celeste loved to sit on hers and watch the spectacular desert sunsets. Only now, she'd have to beware of unwelcome encounters with her new neighbor.

"Nice Pooch." Mia stopped about three feet away, suddenly timid. The dog began thumping his tail furiously.

"Let him smell your hand first. That way he knows you won't hurt him." Celeste crouched next to Pooch and demonstrated. He licked her hand. "It's okay, honey. You can pet him."

Tentatively, Mia reached out. Pooch sniffed her and then rolled onto his back, inviting a belly rub. "He's all bristly, like dry grass," Mia said.

A deep male laugh sounded behind them.

"That's because he's a terrier. They have rough coats, but they're Jell-O inside."

Celeste shot a sharp glance Ray's way, wondering if the allusion to jello had been intentional. He looked absolutely guileless. In fact his expression could only be described as adoring. Why was he looking at Mia that way? Celeste's heartbeat kicked up a notch.

Relax, she told herself. He couldn't know. Except for her dark hair, Mia didn't look a bit like Ray. The high cheekbones could have come from her side of the family, which was mostly English and Scandinavian. And Mia's pale skin and blue-gray eyes were definitely Mom's contribution.

Ray's gaze shifted in her direction. Celeste quickly looked away, embarrassed to be caught studying him.

"Would you like to see the inside? It's not fit for habitation yet, but it might be interesting to get a before and after picture." He held up a Polaroid camera. "Mia can help."

He'd said the magic words. What kid could resist a new toy? Mia stopped petting Pooch and jumped up to tug at her mother's hand. "Please, Mom. I want to see."

How did he always manage to put her in this position? She couldn't very well say no. At least not politely. "Okay, but we can't stay long."

"Yay!"

Ray opened the door and Mia ran in ahead of them. Celeste turned sideways as she scooted past. She couldn't help herself. The proximity of Ray's sun-warmed body, the lock of raven hair that fell into his eyes, his dark, penetrating gaze, all combined to turn her into a sniveling coward.

Safely inside, Celeste took in her surroundings. An involuntary gasp escaped her lips. It was worse than she'd imagined. "*Santos!* What kind of lunatic spray-paints graffiti in his own home?"

"Not much of a decorator, was he? Actually, it looks a lot better than it did this morning. I have six bags of trash in the back of Gus' pickup."

"It smells like cinnamon," Mia said.

Ray touched Mia's nose with his forefinger. "That's right. It smelled so bad when we got here this morning, it made poor Pooch sneeze. I cleaned out the refrigerator and doused the place with air freshener."

Pooch woofed and nudged Mia's hand with his nose.

The little girl knelt and put her arms around the scruffy dog. He stood perfectly still, tongue hanging out and a blissful expression on his face. "Do you think he understands us?"

"It sure seems that way, doesn't it? Come on, I'll give you a tour," Ray said.

They walked through the dining room and into the kitchen. "Whew! I think you could use a little more air freshener in here." Celeste held her nose with two fingers and made a face at Mia.

Ray grinned. "That will make a great picture. Mia, why don't you stand over by the refrigerator with your mom."

Mia and Celeste positioned themselves in front of the open refrigerator, held their noses and made sour lemon faces. Ray clicked. Immediately, a stiff white rectangle shot out the front of the camera. Mia ran over to look.

"It didn't work." Disappointment pinched her features.

Ray knelt beside her, holding the photo. "Wait. In just a few minutes, you'll see the two prettiest girls in Aubrey's Landing."

Celeste felt an unexpected glow of pleasure at the compliment. Don't be such a ninny, she chided herself. He was only joking with Mia. It had been a long time since she'd seen Mia so happy and excited. Her normally shy and serious daughter seemed to blossom in Ray's presence.

She misses her father. The realization hit Celeste like a cold shower. The only male presence in Mia's life was her Grandfather Leander. Although Celeste's father adored the little girl, it wasn't the same as having a daddy. Mia was far too young to understand the circumstances surrounding her father's death, but Celeste couldn't help but wonder if she'd felt the tensions in their home.

"Look, Mom. There you are! You look funny."

Celeste bent down and tickled her daughter's ribs. Mia squirmed and giggled. "Thank you very much, Miss. You look pretty funny yourself."

Ray watched them, an indecipherable expression on his face. He handed the picture to Celeste. "Come on, you two. We have a few more rooms to see."

"Can I take a picture now?" Mia asked.

"You bet. Let me show you how this works." Ray bent down and gave her a quick lesson in point-and-click photography. "How about a picture of your mom and me by the fireplace?"

Mia's eyes sparkled. "Yeah! With the lunatic words."

Celeste laughed. As she joined Ray in front of the stone fireplace, her heart filled with gratitude. Not since the days before her husband's death had her daughter radiated such childish joy and enthusiasm. She swallowed the lump in her throat and smiled at Ray, hoping to convey her thanks. He smiled back and at that moment, Mia snapped the picture.

They took several more photos, of Mia and Pooch, Mia and Ray, Pooch and Ray, and odd subjects that caught the child's interest. Celeste declined to pose again but enjoyed watching her daughter dance around the house, camera in hand and a look of pure delight on her face. Finally, the roll of film was gone.

Ray spread the pictures in a double row on the stone hearth. "I think I may have the next Annie Leibowitz living next door."

"Who's she?" Mia asked.

"Just one of the most famous photographers in the world. I have a book of her photos. When my things arrive from Miami, I'll show it to you."

Mia beamed with pride. She and Celeste admired the photos, picking them up and commenting on each.

"You can keep one if you like," Ray offered.

"Really?" Mia stood back and pondered her choices. "I like this one." She picked up the photo of her mother and Ray.

Celeste felt a queer little pain in her chest. She hoped Mia wasn't getting any ideas. Ray had a way with children. She was grateful he'd made Mia happy, but she had no intention of getting involved with him.

Ray nodded, a grave expression on his face. "Good decision. Your mom is much better looking than Pooch. I bet she doesn't howl either."

Mia thought that over. "No, but sometimes she snores."

Celeste rose quickly. "Say good-bye to Mr. Fontana, Mia."

"Good-bye, Mr. Fontana."

"I'd really like it if you called me Ray. If that's okay with your mom." He glanced at Celeste.

Behind Ray's smile, Celeste thought she caught a hint of sadness. *He's probably just tired. He'd worked hard today.* "Of course. We had a lovely time. Thank you." She took Mia's hand and moved toward the door.

"Before you go, I wanted to ask a favor."

Rats. He wasn't going to let her escape so easily. Warily, she turned. "Yes?"

"Since you're so good at decorating, I was hoping you'd help me pick out a few things for the house. You know, like curtains and furniture . . ." His woeful puppy dog look put Pooch to shame.

Oh no, Celeste thought. She wasn't falling for the old helpless male routine. Ray could go down to the catalog store and pick out curtains just as easily as she could. "I'm sorry, Ray. With my job, committee work, and Mia I really can't spare the time. I hope you understand."

"Sure." Ray walked out on the porch with them. He stood watching until they reached their door. "Be seeing you," he called.

Not if I see you first, Celeste thought.

That night Mia put the photo in a place of honor on her dresser.

In the days and weeks that followed, Celeste and Mia grew accustomed to the sounds of construction from the house next door. Ray invited them over several times but Celeste always made an excuse.

Mia, however, became a regular visitor. Every day when they came home she ran over to pet Pooch and check on Ray's progress. She seemed to enjoy her visits so much that Celeste didn't have the heart to stop them.

In the evening, the sound of hammers, saws, and staple guns was replaced by the rhythmic thump of a punching bag. Ray had been a boxing champion at Arizona Boys Ranch, and evidently had never lost his love for the sport.

Celeste mentally ticked off Ray's activities as she mopped the kitchen floor. He ran the sporting goods store in the morning, worked on his house in the afternoon, and beat that punching bag to a pulp every night in the garage. Plus, he arose at dawn and jogged five days a week.

Where did the man get all that energy? She carried the mop bucket to the backyard and dumped it under the mesquite tree she'd planted last spring. Right now, she could hear Ray's whistled rendition of a show tune as he painted the trim on the side of his house. She paused for a minute, trying to identify it. "I'd Do Anything," from *Oliver.* Feeling pleased, she walked back in the house.

She'd been playing a one-sided game of Name That Tune ever since Ray moved in. As a neighbor, Ray wasn't nearly as bad as she'd feared. In fact, he'd been a perfect gentleman, polite, friendly, and unintrusive. Sometimes she wondered if she'd imagined the passionate kiss they shared in her hallway.

Although she hated to admit it, she derived a strange comfort from knowing Ray was close. He obviously adored Mia, and she him. Celeste knew if she or Mia ever needed anything, Ray would be there to help.

If he stayed. She really knew very little about Ray's recent life, except that he'd been in Miami. What had he done there? she wondered. Was he a carpenter, a handyman, a mechanic?

Celeste walked back outside and gave the bath-room rug a vigorous shake. She tried to get her housecleaning done on Friday evening so she'd be free to enjoy the weekend with Mia.

The smell of simmering green chili, onions, and garlic reminded Celeste it was almost time for dinner. She'd put *chili verde*, pork and green chile stew, in the Crock-Pot this morning. Now if she could just tear Mia away from her new friends.

Celeste washed her hands and smoothed her hair before walking next door. She followed the sound of Ray's whistling, knowing Mia and Pooch would be nearby.

Mia ran over when she saw her mom approach. "Mama, it's finished!"

"What's finished?" Celeste asked.

"Ray's house."

Ray climbed down off a ladder. The fall sun had

toasted his skin to a deep golden brown. Flecks of terra cotta paint clung to his shiny black hair.

Celeste involuntarily took a step backward. Without trying, Ray made her acutely aware of his masculine power and her feminine yearnings. The yin and yang. She supposed he had that effect on a lot of women.

Ray pulled a rag from the back pocket of his faded jeans and wiped his hands. "The major repairs are finished. But I still need to fix up the inside. Come in. I'll show you the curtains I ordered."

Celeste wavered. She didn't want to risk being in close quarters with Ray, but she was dying to see what he'd done with the place. Curiosity won.

She made a slow circle around the living room. "And you said you needed help decorating. This looks wonderful."

Light apricot walls complimented a newly installed oak parquet floor. The rough gray stones of the fireplace were as clean and shiny as river rocks. A card table and two chairs occupied the dining room. The only other furniture consisted of a futon and a television set.

Ray grinned like a five-year-old who'd been told his finger painting was the best in the class. "Do you think so? The lady at the hardware store helped me with the colors."

She'd been feeling a little guilty about refusing to help, but he obviously didn't need her. He'd done just fine by himself. "Absolutely. Now where are those curtains you mentioned?"

"Wait here for just a minute. I'll go get them."

He returned with a brown paper parcel. "I wasn't sure about the color, but I thought since the walls are apricot, I should get something in the same color family. These are nutmeg."

Celeste's mouth dropped open but no sound came out. There were no words to describe the hideousness of the curtains Ray unfolded in front of her. The orangish brown color reminded her of . . . well, she didn't want think about it. The shade certainly didn't resemble any spice she'd ever seen.

Tentatively, she reached out to feel the fabric. Besides being the most atrocious color imaginable, the curtains were thin and unlined. They'd never withstand the afternoon sun's assault on Ray's west-facing living room windows. She'd give them one summer, two at most, before they disintegrated, which might be a blessing for all concerned.

"You don't like them." Ray's face had that puppy dog look again. "I thought nutmeg was another shade of orange, like apricot, only with more brown in it."

"Technically, nutmeg is an umber," Celeste corrected. She couldn't think of a single positive thing to say about those curtains.

"What's umber?" Mia asked.

"It's a reddish-brown, sweetie. Like cinnamon."

"Uh-oh."

In unison, Celeste and Mia turned their attention to Ray.

"I ordered cinnamon curtains for the bedrooms. I guess those won't work either." Ray sank into the futon.

Mia knelt on the floor beside him, sympathy etched on her small features. "Poor Ray." She patted his hand. "You didn't mean to buy ugly curtains."

Even Pooch got into the act. Sensing something wrong, the scruffy tan dog rose from his rug by the fireplace and sat in front of his master, pawing the air and whimpering piteously.

Celeste couldn't stand it. "All right, you guys. It's not the end of the world. Ray, make a list of the things you need and we'll go shopping tomorrow."

The sun broke through the clouds. "Really? I mean, I know you're busy."

She couldn't help smiling at the hopeful look on Ray's face. "I'll make time." For the good of the neighborhood, she added mentally.

"Yay! We're going shopping." Ray grabbed Mia's hands and danced her around the living room. Pooch leaped and barked beside them.

Sheesh. Such excitement over picking out curtains. Mia didn't usually even like shopping but Celeste had the feeling her daughter would adore any activity that included Ray.

*   *   *

Ray tilted his chair against the front of the house, enjoying the quiet, starlit desert evening. He often sat on his front porch until Celeste's lights went out. It made him feel better to know she and Mia were safely tucked into bed before he called it a night.

The day had gone even better than expected. He'd gambled that Celeste would rescue him from utter ineptness as a decorator. What he hadn't counted on was the boost he'd received from Mia and Pooch. Pooch had been rewarded with a juicy marrow bone. He'd buy Mia something at the toy store tomorrow.

Although the rest of his performance was calculated, his elation at Celeste's offer had been genuine. He felt like he'd been handed the world on a platter when she agreed to go shopping with him. Tomorrow, if his luck held out, he'd break through Celeste's defenses and begin a real relationship with her. A relationship like they used to have, before he'd thrown it away.

He hadn't really put his feelings into words until Micah cornered him a couple of weeks ago and demanded to know his intentions. Ray smiled as he watched the lights go out next door. Micah was so protective of Celeste, you'd almost think he was *her* big brother. But that was Micah. He felt responsible for everyone.

He told Micah he intended to marry Celeste. She was his missing piece, the one thing he needed to make his life complete. His successes had left him unfulfilled because he had no one special to share them with. He realized that now. Celeste was the only woman he'd ever truly loved. Soon, she and Mia would be his family.

Micah's second question had been a little trickier. Why hadn't he been honest with Celeste about his recent life? Ray hadn't quite sorted that out himself. It started as a whim. While he was in Aubrey's Landing, he'd wanted to see how people reacted to the old Ray Fontana, town bad boy and boat racer turned mechanic. He'd been surrounded by false friends so long he needed to get away from all the phoniness.

Or maybe it went even deeper. Maybe he needed to return to his roots to find out where he went wrong. Success sure hadn't brought him happiness. If he could win Celeste's love without the help of money, power, or prestige, he'd feel like he finally accomplished something worthwhile.

The front legs of his chair hit the porch with a dull clunk. In any event, he was committed. He'd taken a leave of absence from his duties at Native Spirit Boats. As he explained to Micah, he fully intended to tell Celeste the truth, when the time was right.

Ray whistled softly for Pooch. The dog trotted around the corner of the house. "Come on, old fella. Time for bed." He rubbed the wiry hair behind Pooch's ears, then opened the screen door.

The last few weeks had been some of the happiest of his life. He enjoyed working with his hands and felt proud of the transformation of his new home. He wished he could bring his collection of Native American art from Miami Beach, but then Celeste would know he wasn't quite as clueless as he seemed. Or as poor. One of his antique Navajo rugs was worth more than he'd paid for the entire house.

He walked from room to room, methodically turning out lights. For now, he'd have to be content with discount furniture and catalog curtains. When he convinced Celeste he was worthy of her love and trust, he'd be able to provide both mother and daughter with the luxury they deserved.

Tomorrow could be the start of a new life for all of them.

Chapter Six

They spent Saturday morning looking at furniture and household accessories. Celeste and Mia helped Ray pick out matching shower curtains, rugs, and towels for his bathroom. They selected an inexpensive sofa and a comfortable overstuffed chair in shades of oatmeal, gray, and forest green, with green accent pillows. Finally, they purchased heavy, insulated living room drapes in cream woven with tan threads.

By noon, they'd hit every furniture, department, and discount store in Aubrey's Landing. Ray sensed Mia's enthusiasm was beginning to flag.

He helped Mia and Celeste into the truck's cab, then climbed in beside them. "How about a picnic lunch at the community park? My treat."

Mia turned entreating eyes toward Celeste. She clutched the doll Ray had purchased close to her chest. A box containing a child-size tea set rested on the floorboards. "Can we, Mom? I want to play on the swings and have a tea party with my new doll."

Ray reached across Mia and touched Celeste's hand. "Please. As a small thank-you for all your help."

Celeste hesitated for a moment. "Mia loves the park," she said.

He turned the key in the ignition and fired the old truck to life. "I'll take that as a yes."

They stopped for a take-out chicken dinner, then drove the short distance to Johansen Community Park.

"Looks like we have the place to ourselves," Ray said, climbing out of the truck. A light breeze ruffled the surface of the Colorado River as fluffy white clouds drifted across the sky.

They walked to a covered picnic area that separated the park from a protected cove. Ray guessed this must be a popular place for families in the summertime. The main channel of the river was too deep and swift for inexperienced swimmers, but the cove's shallow beach seemed safe enough for a toddler.

He set boxes containing fried chicken, mashed potatoes and gravy, corn on the cob, and biscuits on a picnic table. Celeste helped unpack before fixing Mia a plate.

"They didn't have anyplace like this when I was growing up here," Ray said between bites of chicken.

"Where did you swim?" Mia asked.

He pointed at the swiftly moving water beyond the levee. "Out there."

Mia's eyes got big. "Weren't you scared?"

"I would have been, except I had someone to take care of me."

"Your mom?"

Ray laughed. "My mother would have been very upset if she'd known where I was." He lowered his voice to a stage whisper. "Sometimes I went to the river when I was supposed to be in school."

"Really?" Mia's eyes grew even wider. Her plate sat in front of her, forgotten.

Ray nodded. "I was a very naughty boy, but Beauty kept me safe."

"Who's Beauty?"

"She was the smartest, kindest, most beautiful dog in the world, and the best swimmer. She'd paddle across the river with me holding onto her tail."

He caught a warning glance from Celeste.

"Of course, I was a lot older than you. Practically a teenager. I would never, ever have gone to the river by myself when I was seven."

"I should hope not." Celeste reached across the table to brush a tiny crumb from Mia's chin. "Eat your lunch so you can play, sweetie."

Mia nibbled at her corn. "Did she look like Pooch?"

"No, Beauty was pure black with a white diamond on her chest. She loved the water more than any dog I've ever seen."

"Where is she now?" Mia asked.

"I think she's in heaven."

Mia nodded gravely. "Like my daddy." She took a last bite of potatoes, then turned to her mother. "Can I play now?"

Celeste looked at Mia's half-eaten lunch and sighed. "I guess. I'll save the rest of your lunch. Maybe you'll want more later."

They watched the child scamper to the playground. "That breeze is a little cool. I think I'll get Mia's sweater out of the truck." Celeste stood but Ray put a restraining hand on her arm.

"She'll be fine. Sit and talk with me for a while." He patted the seat next to him. "You can see Mia better from this side."

Celeste perched on the farthest end of his bench. Her gray eyes regarded him warily. "What about?"

"How about local history?" It was the safest topic he could come up with on short notice. He had the feeling that unless he proceeded cautiously, he might lose this precious opportunity to bridge the distance between them. "I was wondering how this park got its name."

Celeste seemed to relax a little. At least, she didn't look ready to bolt from her seat. "It was named for Silas Johansen, my great-grandfather. He was a steamship captain on the Colorado River. Years ago, the ships stopped right here to load crops grown by farmers in Parker Valley. They took the produce upriver to feed soldiers at Fort Mojave."

"I've heard about the steamships. The captains hired Yuman Indians to guide them around rock bars in the river."

"That's right."

Ray got up and began clearing the remains of their picnic from the table. "Hey, maybe our great-grandfathers worked together."

Celeste laughed. For goodness sakes, what was she so nervous about? Ray presented no threat, at least not in the middle of the afternoon at Johansen Park. She waved at Mia, sitting at the top of the slide. "We don't know much about each other, do we?"

"I guess we don't." Ray rejoined her at the picnic table. Was it her imagination, or had he edged a little closer? He turned to face her, a teasing smile on his firm and oh-so-kissable lips. "What would you like to know? Ask me anything."

Celeste jerked her gaze away from Ray's mouth. She'd wanted to learn more about the mysterious Ray Fontana since the day he appeared in the hospital cafeteria. She couldn't let this opportunity pass. "Anything?"

Ray looked amused. "Anything."

"Well, I did wonder about your life in Miami. Like where you worked for instance."

"That's easy. I worked for Native Spirit Boats."

"Oh. Were you a mechanic?"

"Among other things."

"Why did you leave?"

"Ahh, now we get to the hard stuff." Ray stared at the swiftly flowing river. "I guess I felt like something was missing from my life. When I came back to Aubrey's Landing, I thought I might find it here." His piercing gaze settled on Celeste. "So I decided to stick around for a while."

She shifted uncomfortably on the hard wooden bench. "This isn't a permanent move, then?"

"Gus has offered to keep me on at the Bait Shop. I might be able to buy it from him in a year or two. It all depends."

Relief surged through her. She felt like she could float to the tops of the weeping willow trees whose graceful branches swept the riverbank. A prick of suspicion brought her down to earth again. "On what?"

Ray grinned. "I can't reveal all my secrets. You'd think I was boring. By the way, did I mention that I expect quid pro quo?"

"What?" She was having trouble keeping up

with this conversation, and her wildly shifting emotions.

"You know, tit for tat. One good story deserves another."

Celeste laughed. "How long have you been in Aubrey's Landing? Six weeks? Surely you've heard all about me by now."

Ray faced the sunlight. Maybe that explained the hooded look in his dark eyes. "Even small towns keep secrets."

Cool, calm, and collected. Celeste repeated her mantra for moments when panic threatened to overwhelm her. Ray obviously hadn't guessed *her* secret and she didn't intend to tell him.

She attempted a light, bantering tone. "All right. I asked you three questions so I'll answer three. Tit for tat."

Ray gave her his familiar sardonic grin. "I'm not sure your arithmetic is accurate, but I accept. Question number one. What's this committee work you mentioned?"

Ah, safe territory, at least for now. "We're planning an obstetrics center for women who aren't able to pay for prenatal care and a safe hospital delivery. Unfortunately, getting the financing has been harder than we thought. It looks like it will be a long time before our dream becomes a reality."

"It sounds like a good cause. I'm surprised people aren't jumping at the chance to help."

"Aubrey's Landing isn't a wealthy community. Those who are able to contribute have many worthy causes competing for their dollars."

"How about your father? Seems like he'd be the perfect patron for an obstetrics center, seeing as how he delivered about half the town."

Celeste sighed. "Father has a tendency to want to control things. The committee approached him a year ago, but he didn't agree with their fundraising methods, the proposed site for the center, the architectural plans, the staffing . . ."

"Sounds like he disagreed with just about everything."

"You've got it. My father has always been a little inflexible, and the stroke seemed to accentuate that aspect of his personality. Anyway, the committee decided they couldn't work with him."

"That must have been difficult for you."

Celeste shrugged. "I'm used to my father's eccentricities. I try not to let his actions or opinions affect me."

"Prove it."

Celeste had been watching Mia swing. She snapped her head in Ray's direction so quickly she almost got whiplash. "What?"

"Prove that your father's opinions don't affect you by going out to dinner with me."

Ohhhh. So that's what Ray had been leading up to. He looked almost boyish, sitting there with a hopeful expression on his face and that stubborn lock of black hair falling across his forehead. He reminded her of the young man she'd known eight years ago. The man who said he loved her, then left without a word.

"I'm sorry, Ray. As I told you before, I really don't have the time or inclination to start a relationship."

To her surprise, Ray didn't seem the least bit offended. The expression in his dark eyes held tenderness and something else. Could it be pity?

"Don't you get lonely?" he asked.

Only during sultry summer nights when a raven-haired man visited her dreams. Or on Sunday afternoons when she and Mia watched other families at the park. She couldn't help wondering what it would be like to be part of a loving family. But that didn't seem to be in the cards for her and Mia. Better to be grateful for what they had than risk everything on a man.

Celeste brushed her hair back from her forehead. "I have friends and work and Mia. And . . . and Rosa." *Santos,* why did she feel the need to justify her life? And why was she trembling?

Unable to contain her agitation, she rose from the bench. "Believe it or not, it's quite possible to have a full and satisfying life without a husband."

Ray gazed up at her, his expression inscrutable. When he spoke, his voice was gentle. "I didn't ask you to marry me, angel. I only asked you to dinner."

Celeste wished she could join the ants scurrying away with crumbs from their picnic. She sunk down on the bench, one hand pressed to her flaming cheek. "What I meant to say was, I don't date."

"How is Rosa?"

Celeste blinked rapidly. "Rosa?"

"Right."

Ray had deliberately changed the subject. Was he unwilling to accept her refusal? Or just being kind? Either way, she welcomed the reprieve. "Rosa's fine. She takes care of Mia after school every day."

"Rosa says you have big *huevos.*" Mia's small piping voice interrupted.

The two adults turned to look at her. She stood on the opposite side of the picnic table. "We have big eggs too. We buy the extra large kind at the grocery store. Big *huevos* are good, aren't they?"

Ray grinned at Celeste. "I guess that depends on what you do with them."

"Pancakes!" Celeste hopped up from the table and began gathering the leftovers. "We make pancakes with our eggs, don't we, Mia? Which reminds me, I need to go to the grocery store."

Mia's little face fell. "Do we have to go, Mom? I want to have a tea party with you and Ray."

"I'm sorry, sweetie. We really do. Patti and Rowena are coming over this evening. We can have a tea party with them."

"Can Ray come too?"

Celeste cast an uneasy glance in his direction. "I think Ray will be busy . . . fixing up his house."

Ray patted the child's shoulder. "Maybe next time, princess."

"She said *what?*"

"Shhh!" Celeste glanced toward the bedroom where the little girls played. In a low tone, she repeated Mia's comment. "I thought she'd forgotten all about it."

"Hah! No such luck. Kids tuck these things away until the most embarrassing moment. Then they spring them on you."

Celeste and Patti sat on the living room carpet, cutting Halloween shapes out of brightly colored construction paper. Patti added an orange jack-o-lantern to the pile on the coffee table. "I think Rosa's right. Figuratively speaking, of course. Ray strikes me as a man who knows what he wants and goes after it."

Celeste carefully cut around a witch's broomstick. "That's what scares me."

Patti put down her scissors and took a sip from an icy glass of lemonade. "I wonder if it's Ray who scares you, or your own feelings?"

"Maybe a little of both." Celeste met her friend's sympathetic gaze. "Okay, maybe a lot of both."

"How long has it been since you've been on a date?"

The question caught Celeste off guard. "I, well, I haven't dated. Not since Blake died."

"No wonder you're confused." Patti set her glass down on a rose-colored coaster. "The best way to find out if it's really Ray you want is to play the field. Go out with someone else."

Celeste blinked. Of course, it made perfect sense. She was lonely and vulnerable. That's why she'd been unable to control her emotions around Ray. There was only one problem. "Who?"

"How about that good-looking doctor who's always hanging around you? Dr. Band-Aid."

"You mean Dr. Bandini."

"Whatever. He certainly seems eager."

Inwardly, Celeste cringed. The thought of a evening with Gorgeous George didn't exactly make her quiver with anticipation. But, what the heck, he was male and available. And she was desperate. "I'll do it," she said.

Patti gave her the thumbs-up sign. "Good for you. Let's break out the ice cream and celebrate."

"Not so fast. I'd like to hear what's up with you and a certain handsome but shy minister."

Patti sat back on her haunches. "Nada. A big zip. I've done everything I can think of to let Micah know I'm interested but he doesn't seem to get it. Maybe he just isn't attracted to me."

Celeste shook her head. "I've seen the way he looks at you when he thinks no one's watching. I wouldn't give up. In the meantime, maybe you should take your own advice."

"Been there, done that," Patti said. "I know who I want, and it isn't Jack the pool man or Ernie the electrician. Now, if you don't mind, I think I'll go drown my sorrows in Rocky Road."

"I'm right behind you."

A little while later, the girls joined them at the dining room table. They looked like two kittens who'd just polished off a dish of cream. What were they up to? Celeste wondered. If Mia and Rowena weren't such good little girls, she might be worried.

Before Rowena went home that evening, Celeste saw the girls exchange a pinkie handshake, reserved for the most solemn occasions.

On second thought, maybe she should worry.

"Did you see that match last night between Felix Gonzales and Miguel Antonio Jimenez?" Clarence posed the question from the depths of his brown naugahyde recliner, strategically positioned under the bulletin board in the Bait Shop garage. Pooch lounged on an old blanket at his feet.

Ray grinned to himself as he cleaned the carburetor on a Mercury outboard. *Here we go,* he thought. *Round One.*

Gus threw the first punch. "I did and it was a disgrace. Gonzales had him on the ropes in the fifth round. That pretty boy Jimenez must have winked at one of the judges. You'd think it was a gol-durn beauty contest, the way he pranced around the ring."

Glancing over his shoulder, Ray caught Gus' exaggerated imitation of a beauty contestant's walk from the soda pop machine to the bulletin board and back again.

Nurse Wilmer had switched to swing shift so she could check on Gus every morning. Although the old cuss would rather give up a ringside seat at a title match than admit it, Ray suspected he enjoyed sparring with her. The formidable nurse had somehow cajoled or coerced Gus into attending nutrition classes and working out three days a week under the supervision of the hospital's cardiac rehab staff.

As for Nurse Wilmer, what had started as a challenge and the chance to earn a little extra money seemed to be evolving into a genuine friendship.

Clarence lumbered up from his recliner. "Why, that boy has more finesse in his little finger than Gonzales has in his whole scraggly body. Did you see those right hooks?" Clarence demonstrated, clutching the unsmoked cigar in his left hand while he swung with his right. "He's the finest featherweight boxer to ever come out of Tijuana."

Gus snorted. "Which ain't saying much."

"Oye, Ray. You have company."

Ray's new employee stood in the doorway. Mia and Rowena peeked from behind the kid, looking like they'd stumbled into an alien land.

"Thank you, Manuel."

The boy hitched up his baggy trousers, waved a tattooed hand, and headed back into the store.

"Welcome, ladies. Come on in." Ray wiped his hands on a rag and motioned for the girls to enter. He led them to the corner that held the soda pop machine and Senior Citizen Day Care Center. "Mia and Rowena, these are my friends, Gus and Clarence." Pooch stood, stretched, and welcomed the girls with a wagging tail.

"Howdy-do, ladies," said Clarence.

Gus nodded. "Pleased to meet you."

The little girls greeted them shyly, then busied themselves petting Pooch. Finally, Rowena spoke. "Why were you fighting?" she asked.

Clarence sank into the recliner, his cheeks pink from exertion. He dug his hands into the pockets of his overalls. "Heck, we weren't fighting. We were just . . . exercising."

"These two love to argue. It's their hobby. Sort of like playing checkers." Ray put some quarters in the pop machine. "What'll it be girls, lemon-lime, strawberry, or root beer?"

"I'll have root beer, please," said Rowena.

Mia stood slightly behind her friend, one hand resting on Pooch's head. Her voice barely rose above a whisper. "Strawberry, please."

"Sit right down here." Gus whipped out his handkerchief and dusted the seats on two castoff dining room chairs. "Looks like you've been to the library."

The girls perched on their seats, balancing stacks of books in their laps. "Umm-hmm," said Rowena over the top of her root beer.

They daintily sipped their sodas while the old timers rubbed their scratchy chins and gazed into the distance. Neither pair seemed to know what to say to the other.

What were the girls doing here by themselves? Ray wondered. They obviously had something on their minds. He hadn't seen much of Mia or Celeste since last weekend. Usually, he'd be home by now, but on this particular Wednesday afternoon he had a tune-up to finish. "Would you like to see some water dogs?" he asked.

Mia leaped to her feet, barely managing to hang on to her books. "You becha!"

Everyone looked in surprise at the reserved little girl, who until now had hung behind her older friend.

Ray laughed. "Let's go then."

He lead the girls into the store, where Manuel emptied rolls of change into the cash register. "How's it going?" Ray asked.

"I had four sales this morning."

"Not bad for the second week in October. Keep up the good work."

Manuel flashed him a proud-but-shy grin. "Okay, boss."

Hiring Manuel had been the best thing he'd done since he came back to Aubrey's Landing, other than moving next door to Celeste and Mia. The kid reminded him of himself at that age. Manuel had been on the edge, too, involved in a gang, in trouble with the police. Then he got his girlfriend pregnant and decided to go straight. When he hired Manuel, Ray felt like he'd been given the chance to pay a long overdue debt.

Ray stopped in front of two large rectangular bait tanks in the right rear corner of the store. "Here we are. Water Dog Central."

Mia and Rowena bent down to peer at the muddy brown salamanders. Several swam close to the front of the tank, waving their tiny, useless front legs. "Look! They have whiskers," said Rowena.

"What are their names?" Mia asked.

Ray cleared his throat. How could he tell the little girl who looked at him with big innocent eyes that he sold these water dogs for bait? "Actually, we haven't named them yet. We let their new owners do that. Would you like to take one home with you?"

The girls looked at him like he'd just offered them an all-expense paid trip to Disney World.

"Really? asked Mia.

"Me too?" said Rowena.

"Of course, you too." Ray felt like Santa Claus. It took so little to thrill kids. He just hoped their moms liked salamanders. "We'll put them in baggies for you to take home. I'll even throw in some food. But first, I think you girls have something you want to tell me."

The girls looked at each other and then at Ray.

"Like why you're here instead of at the library?"

Rowena nudged Mia with her elbow. "It's about my mom," Mia began.

Fear knifed through him. He hadn't seen Celeste for several days. He'd been working late, doing inventory with Gus and Manuel, but he'd watched her lights go off at the usual time. "Is something wrong?" he asked. "She's not sick, is she?"

"Yes. I mean, no. She's not sick. She's going to play the field with Dr. Band-Aid and we don't want her to because we like you." The words came out in a rush. Mia pushed the hair back from her forehead, unconsciously mimicking her mom's habitual gesture.

It took a moment for Mia's words to register. So Celeste didn't date. At least not until this Dr. Band-Aid asked her.

Jealousy twisted his gut. He rose quickly, determined to hide his hurt and disappointment from the girls. "Your mom's a grownup, Mia. She has the right to date anybody she likes."

Rowena jumped in. "We think Celeste likes you, but she's afraid. We want to help you win her, like Ivanhoe won Lady Rowena."

Ray smiled at his champions. "This wouldn't involve galloping toward Dr. Band-Aid with a lance, would it? Because I'm afraid I don't own a horse and I'd look pretty silly running at Dr. Band-Aid with this fishing pole." He hoisted a pole under his arm to demonstrate.

Mia giggled. "My mom likes bubble bath and chocolates."

"And romance novels," added Rowena

"And love poems." Mia rolled her eyes and made a face.

Ray couldn't help but grin. "Okay, I get the picture. Romantic stuff."

"Right," said Rowena

"Right," echoed Mia.

"I'll keep that in mind. Now let's get those water dogs bagged up and take you back to the library before your moms start to worry."

Chapter Seven

Too late. Ray spotted Celeste and Rosa across the street at the public library. Even from this distance, he recognized the worried frown on Celeste's face.

"Uh-oh," said Rowena. "We're in trouble."

Ray raised a hand and waved. "Over here," he shouted. Then, in a lower tone of voice, "Let me handle this, girls."

They walked to the corner and, after looking both ways, trooped across the street. The little girls balanced their library books in the crook of their arms. With their free hands, they grasped the water-filled baggies containing their new pets.

"Sorry we're late. I invited the girls in for a soda, wc got to talking and, I guess the time got away from us." Ray offered an apologetic grin. "Hello, Rosa."

The older woman nodded but did not smile. Her dark eyes bored into him. Ray had the uncomfortable feeling she could see to the depths of his none-too-pure soul.

"I should have realized where they'd gone. Girls, don't ever do that again. You scared us to death." Celeste stooped to give each of the girls a hug. Suddenly, she squealed and jumped back. "What on earth is that?" She pointed at the muddy brown amphibian, who waved at her through the plastic baggy.

"It's a water dog, Mom. Can I keep him, please? He doesn't bite or anything."

Ray maintained a straight face. "They make great pets. Very low maintenance." He took Celeste's arm to steady her as she advanced cautiously to examine the creatures, then held on a little longer than necessary, savoring the warm, silky feel of her skin.

Celeste's cheeks turned seashell pink. She backed away from him and rubbed her arm, as if his touch had burned her. Trouble roiled in the depths of her blue-gray eyes.

"Can I, Mom?"

"What?" Celeste turned to her daughter. "I guess so. Tell Ray thank you, girls. We need to go home."

To Ray's surprise and delight, Mia and Rowena

nearly bowled him over with gratitude. He stooped to return their hugs.

"Thank you," said Rowena.

"It's the best pet I ever had." Mia started to join her mother, then turned back abruptly. "Is it a boy or a girl?"

Ray considered for a moment. "It's hard to tell with water dogs. What do you think?"

Mia held the baggy up to her face, studying her pet eye to eye. "It's a girl," she announced with finality. "I'm going to name her Beauty."

Ray saw Celeste and Rosa exchange an amused glance. The little salamander was anything but beautiful.

Rowena followed Mia's example, maintaining eye contact with her salamander until inspiration struck. "Mine's a boy," she said. "His name is Ivanhoe."

"Thank you for taking care of the girls." Celeste turned and began to walk toward her car. Mia and Rowena followed but Rosa lingered behind.

"I think you are a coyote in the clothes of a sheep," she hissed.

"It was nice to see you too, Rosa."

The older woman muttered something under her breath, crossed herself and hurried down the sidewalk.

* * *

"I do not trust him." Rosa sat at Celeste's dining room table, sipping a cup of tea. The sound of water running in the bathtub told them Mia was temporarily out of earshot. "I think he is hiding something."

Celeste slipped the casserole she'd prepared the night before into the oven. She straightened and looked at her mamacita. "It doesn't matter, because I'm not interested in Ray, anyway."

Rosa shook her head. Setting down her cup, she tapped the weathered skin under one deep-set eye. "I see the way he looks at you. And I see you try not to look back. It's not easy, is it my Celestina?"

Celeste sighed. She pulled open the refrigerator door and got out the salad makings. "You're too smart. I do have feelings for Ray. And Mia adores him. He's been kind and considerate, a perfect gentleman. I think maybe he's changed."

"Does a puma become a house cat?"

Celeste held the lettuce under running water. How did she get into the position of defending Ray? It reminded her of the arguments she'd had with her father the summer she and Ray dated. He'd been adamantly opposed to their relationship but for once in her life, she'd stood up to him.

Ray wasn't the good-for-nothing her father claimed. She'd seen kindness and vulnerability beneath the dangerous, thrill-seeking exterior. In truth, she saw it still.

"Will you tell him about Mia?"

Celeste froze for a moment, then pushed the knife through a radish, careful to keep her fingers out of the way. "No. I can't take that chance." She added a handful of radishes to the salad greens she'd tossed in a wooden bowl. "Anyway, I've accepted a dinner date with Dr. Bandini this Friday night."

"I've heard about this doctor. He is *muy guapo,* very handsome, no?"

"You could say that." Celeste continued to chop vegetables, avoiding Rosa's penetrating gaze.

"I've heard he has many girlfriends, and he is prettier than most of them."

Celeste couldn't help laughing. She scooped the rest of the ingredients into the salad, then dried her hands. "And he smells sweeter too."

Rosa came around the table to fold her in a hug. "Never mind, Celestina. It's a start. At least this doctor is no puma. Your father will be happy."

Father. Celeste hadn't considered this benefit to dating Giorgio Bandini. Ever since Ray moved in next door, her father had been driving her crazy. She lifted her head from Rosa's shoulder. "By all means, tell him. Maybe he'll quit worrying about me."

When she arrived at the hospital early Thursday morning, a small gift basket wrapped in pink cellophane waited in front of her office. Gripping her lunch bag in her teeth, Celeste picked up the basket and unlocked the door.

With fumbling fingers, she pulled off the curly gold ribbon. One by one, she examined the treasures inside. Jasmine bubble bath, sea mist moisturizing soap, and a small box of Godiva chocolates. But no card.

Who had sent such a thoughtful gift? Could it have been Ray? The thought filled her with a delicious, tingling warmth.

The ringing phone jarred her out of her daydream. When she answered, a deep male voice sounded on the other end. "Good morning, beautiful lady."

Celeste's shoulders slumped. Dr. Bandini. Of course, he'd sent the basket. What a silly goose she was. She strove to keep the disappointment from her voice. "Dr. Bandini. How are you this morning?"

"I'm fine. Better than fine, actually. I'm looking forward to a very special dinner date on Friday. I wanted to call and wish you a day filled with sweet anticipation."

"Oh. Well . . . thank you. I appreciate your thoughtfulness."

"Until Friday, then."

"Until Friday."

He'll probably expect me to fall all over him with gratitude, Celeste thought. She dumped the bubble bath and scented soap back into the basket, then opened the box of candy.

Mmmm. The dense, rich flavor of a chocolate

raspberry truffle captivated her taste buds. At least the doctor knew how to pick chocolates. She had to give him that.

Every morning that week, she found a similar basket outside her door, with sweet-smelling gifts, chocolates, and even a book of love poems. By the end of the week she was beginning to wonder if she'd misjudged the doctor. Someone so thoughtful couldn't be all bad.

"Mr. Bandini?" The fresh-faced hostess appeared at their side with menus in hand. "Your table is ready."

"That's *Doctor* Bandini." Giorgio Bandini rose from his barstool and glowered at the hostess. "And it's about time. Our reservations were for six p.m."

The young woman looked him over coolly, apparently unfazed by his peevishness. "I'm very sorry, Dr. Bandini, but you requested a window table and one has just become available. I think you'll find the view is worth the wait. This way, please." She turned and strode into the restaurant.

Dr. Bandini made an unattractive noise in his throat, somewhere between a snort and a huff. He grasped Celeste's elbow firmly. Together, they sprinted after the hostess, who apparently didn't want to spend a moment longer than necessary in the doctor's company.

Celeste knew how she felt. She fixed her eyes on

the rough hardwood floors, concentrating on keeping her balance in high heels. Whatever had possessed her to think this was a good idea? So far this evening, Dr. Bandini had bored her with the details of his medical achievements, received a well-deserved ticket for speeding, and offended everyone he came in contact with. And that was all before dinner.

The hostess paused in front of a table for two with a lovely view of Lake Havasu. From their vantage point on a bluff overlooking the lake, Celeste saw an armada of jet skis and wave runners.

"This is lovely. Thank you." She gave the hostess an apologetic smile and sank into her chair, praying she wouldn't run into anyone she knew. McGee's was located in Lake Havasu City, Arizona, about thirty miles from Aubrey's Landing. It was the nicest restaurant in the area, and also the most expensive. She'd only been here once before, for a coworker's fiftieth birthday party.

"We'd like a bottle of California Chardonnay, chilled." Dr. Bandini issued the request in a peremptory tone. He placed a hand on Celeste's shoulder. "Excuse me, dear. I need to freshen up."

Dear? Since when am I his dear? She managed not to shrug off his hand, but just barely.

"Your husband seems a little out of sorts tonight." The hostess' expression was amused but sympathetic as she handed Celeste a menu.

"Oh, he's not . . ." Celeste stopped. Why not have a little fun? She leaned forward and spoke in a conspiratorial tone. "The truth is, he's constipated. It always makes him cranky."

The hostess broke into a grin. "Well, that explains it."

"What do you recommend?" Celeste asked as she unfolded her menu.

"I really like the salmon in a pastry shell. And for your husband, a nice big Caesar salad." The hostess unfurled a snowy napkin and placed it Celeste's lap. "Lots of roughage," she whispered.

The women were giggling when Dr. Bandini returned to the table. The hostess cast an amused glance over her shoulder as she made a quick exit.

"What was that about?" Dr. Bandini regarded Celeste disapprovingly.

So much for having fun. She turned her attention to the menu. "I asked her for dinner recommendations."

The doctor shot her an annoyed glance, but didn't press for an explanation. He's probably on his good behavior for our first date, she thought. Hah! She'd hate to see his bad behavior.

The wine arrived, chilled to the doctor's satisfaction. After a couple of glasses, he loosened up considerably. Celeste didn't need to participate in the conversation. Dr. Bandini, or Giorgio, as he insisted she call him, seemed quite content with a nod or comment now and then. On and on he droned, about his years at med school, where he was at the head of his class, his residency in Chicago and how he was cheated out of the chief resident position due to the jealousy and vindictiveness of the teaching staff.

I'm sure it didn't have anything to do with your personality, Celeste thought. She sipped her wine and glanced out the window as a couple on a wave runner sped by, shooting a white plume of spray behind them.

That looks like fun. The thought startled her. Speed had always frightened her, but with the right partner, with someone she trusted. . . . Her vision grew hazy as she imagined Ray on the front of the wave runner, his black hair blowing in the wind. She wrapped her arms around his waist and laid her cheek against his sun-warmed back, enjoying the exhilarating sensation of flying over the water. His abdominal muscles rippled under her fingers as the wave runner hit a wake.

Ray had the hardest body she'd ever seen, carved by physical labor, jogging, and beating that punching bag into submission almost every evening. When he worked outside without a shirt she couldn't keep her eyes off his smoothly muscled torso.

Celeste took a sip of wine and resisted the impulse to fan herself with her napkin. It had suddenly become very warm in the restaurant. Her thoughts returned to Ray with alarming frequency lately. When had she become so lecherous? She tried to focus on what Giorgio was saying. Something about a contract dispute with the hospital?

"Don't you agree?" he asked.

Celeste blinked. "Ummm," she replied, as non-committally as possible.

The waiter appeared, saving her from any further discussion. Giorgio broke off in mid-rant. "I didn't order that." He gestured angrily at the Caesar salad the waiter placed in front of him.

"Compliments of the house, sir." The waiter glanced at Celeste, and for just an instant, she caught a twinkle in his eye. She stifled a grin. The staff was having a little joke at the doctor's expense. She hoped they hadn't mixed powdered laxative into his salad dressing.

"It better not be on the bill." Giorgio picked up his fork and stabbed a big, dripping mouthful.

"And for the lady?"

On second thought, maybe a little Ex-Lax wouldn't be such a bad idea. "Nothing for me, thank you. I'll wait for dinner."

Their entrées followed shortly. Celeste enjoyed her salmon almost as much as the reprieve from Giorgio's monologue. By the time they finished their meal, the sunset had cast a rosy glow on the lake.

"Thank you," Celeste said. "It was a delicious dinner, and what a lovely setting." She gestured toward the pink mountains reflected in the luminous water below their window. Across the lake, tourists strolled through the collection of curio shops and English-themed pubs and restaurants that nestled under the London Bridge. The historic stone bridge had been brought over from Great Britain in the early 1970s and reassembled on the shores of Lake Havasu.

Giorgio Bandini gazed at her like a striped bass sizing up a minnow. His big brown eyes glistened with desire, while a dab of marinara sauce glistened on his chin.

Celeste forged ahead. "I also want to thank you for the lovely gift baskets." There, she'd done it. Her social responsibilities were fulfilled, the check had arrived, and boy, was she ready to go home. She pulled the napkin from her lap and placed it on the table.

Dr. Bandini didn't seem to hear her. His oily gaze rested momentarily on her face, then slid downward to her chest. His voice dropped to a seductive croon as he placed his hand over hers. "May we continue the evening at my condo?"

Celeste suppressed a shudder. She pulled her hand free and stood. "I really have to go home. The babysitter will be waiting for me," Celeste lied. He didn't need to know Mia was spending the night with Patti and Rowena.

Dr. Bandini stood slowly, his expression indulgent. He shook his head. "You see? It's just as I told you. You need to relax and have a little fun."

Celeste leveled a cool stare at him. "I need to go home," she repeated. "Now."

He chuckled, as if she were a foolish but headstrong child. "Very well. I will take you home."

By the time they reached Aubrey's Landing, the evening had turned to night. A slender crescent moon hung above the horizon. Celeste gave half an ear to Giorgio's sad story about his ex-wife. She'd heard it all before. Hospital scuttlebutt said Dr. Bandini had tired of his wife soon after she put him through medical school. When he divorced her, he had the bad luck to draw a female judge who'd suffered a similar fate at the hands of her ex-husband. The doctor's monthly alimony payments were rumored to be about three times the average hospital worker's salary.

Poor, poor Dr. Bandini. Celeste gathered her purse and grasped the door handle, ready to jump out the minute Giorgio brought his forty-thousand-dollar luxury sedan to a halt. If she didn't get out of there soon, she just might tell the doctor what she thought of him, and that wouldn't be good for their working relationship. She'd already made the mother of all mistakes by agreeing to go out with him. Why compound the problem by calling him a pompous, arrogant, insensitive, boorish, miserly nincompoop?

Actually that was going easy on him. If she had another five minutes, she could probably think up ten or twelve more adjectives to describe Giorgio Bandini. Mercifully, it looked as though she wouldn't have to spend that long in the doctor's company.

"Thank you, Giorgio. It was a delightful dinner." *At least the food and the atmosphere were delightful.* She was halfway out of the car before he turned off the ignition.

"Let me walk you to the door," he called.

"No, no, that won't be necessary." Celeste hurried up the front walk, pausing only long enough to wave. "Thanks again. Good night." Then she half ran through the inky blackness as fast as her two-inch heels would carry her. *Drat.* She'd forgotten to turn on the porch light. As she fumbled for the right key she heard Giorgio come up the steps.

"I insist."

Warm breath on her neck told her he was standing close. Too close. Her body stiffened as his hands massaged her shoulders.

"You are so tense. Let me help you relax." The words were followed by a wet kiss on her earlobe.

Celeste spun to face him, knocking his arms away. "Take your hands off me." She used her iciest voice, enunciating each syllable.

Giorgio laughed, an unpleasant sound. He had her pinned against the door. His wine-laced breath fanned her face and his hand came up to caress the back of her neck. Suddenly, he grabbed a handful of hair and tilted back her head. "I think the Ice Princess needs some heat." His voice was low and threatening.

Celeste went very still, offering no resistance. As wet, squishy lips descended on hers, she brought a spiked heel down hard on Giorgio's instep. When he yelped and jumped back she lunged forward, striking him in the nose with the flat of her palm. Then she shifted the keys to her right hand, and waited. She didn't want to jab them in his eyes but she would if he came at her again.

It wasn't necessary. Strong hands seized the doctor from behind and spun him around. Even in the darkness, she could see the fury in Ray's eyes.

"I think it's time for you to go home." He bit out the words between tightly compressed lips. Celeste was sure it took every ounce of his willpower to keep from beating the doctor like a punching bag. He gave Giorgio a hard shove toward the black sedan parked at the curb.

Bandini stumbled a few steps but managed to keep his footing. He half ran, half limped to the car, holding a handkerchief to his bloody nose. When he'd put the length of the yard and his car between them, Giorgio turned and glared at Celeste. "You led me on when you had another man waiting for you," he accused. "You're a tease, a no-good . . ."

Ray advanced on him with a muttered curse, hands balled into fists at his sides. Dr. Giorgio Bandini scrambled into the car, pressed the button to lock his doors and roared off into the autumn night.

Up and down the block, porch lights went on as neighbors poked their head out to see what was causing the commotion. Ray stood in the middle of the sidewalk leading to her door, looking after the doctor's car.

"Ray?" As the adrenaline left her system, Celeste suddenly felt weak. Her voice didn't sound at all like her, she thought. It sounded thin and sort of watery, like undercooked cream of wheat.

Instantly, Ray was by her side, the murderous gleam in his eye replaced by a look of concern. He gently pried the keys from her fist and then, in one swift movement, hoisted her into his arms. "Come on, slugger. Let's get you in the house."

Celeste wanted to protest but the warmth of his hard masculine body felt so wonderful that she couldn't find the strength. Instead, she put her arms around his neck and nuzzled her face into his shoulder. For just a moment, she closed her eyes, savoring the feeling of being loved and protected.

Ray opened the door, turning on the track lighting in the living room. He set Celeste down on one of the oak dining chairs. "Put your head between your knees," he ordered.

Celeste gaped at him. "I'm fine really. Just a delayed reaction." She attempted a smile, but in truth, she was still feeling a little shaky.

"Humor me," he said.

Although Ray seemed calm enough, Celeste noticed the jagged scar above his left eye stood out in stark contrast to his face. Obediently, she lowered her head to her knees.

"Now take some deep breaths."

As she sat contemplating the dining room carpet, breathing in and out, she heard the gurgling sound of the water dispenser in her kitchen. Sneaking a peek, she watched Ray place the tea kettle on the back burner. Then he joined her at the table.

"Can I sit up now?" she asked meekly.

"I think so."

As she unfolded from her crouched position, Celeste saw Ray watching her with such tenderness, it made her heart ache. Had anyone ever looked at her like that before? she wondered. Rosa, maybe, but somehow it wasn't quite the same.

"What on earth possessed you to go out with that imbecile?"

The warm glow Celeste had experienced evaporated. Confused by Ray's sudden change of tone, she stammered the first thing that came to her mind. "He . . . he sent me gift baskets." As soon as the words were out of her mouth she regretted them. What would Ray think of her, accepting a date with that creep because he gave her gifts?

"The baskets had chocolate and bubble bath and poetry. They were really sweet and thoughtful." Ray continued to stare at her, his expression unreadable. She stumbled on, her face burning. "I mean, everyone knows he's a ladies' man, but I thought I saw some good in him."

Ray reached across the table and took her hand. He pressed it to his lips, sending shivers of delight to the very tips of her toes. "My angel," he murmured. "You see good in everyone. Even in people unworthy of your trust."

The whistling of the tea kettle made her jump. She crossed to the stove, glad for a few minutes to collect her thoughts. "I have chamomile tea or instant hot chocolate."

"I'll try the hot chocolate."

She grinned. "I can see you haven't lost your taste for sweets."

Or for you, Ray thought. He'd been sitting outside with his chair tilted back against the house, feeling like a stalker as he waited for Celeste to come home. He'd tried watching television, reading a book, pacing from one room to the next, but his thoughts were a jumble of jealousy, fear, and the old feelings of self-doubt.

Finally, he couldn't stand it any longer. He took his usual seat on the front porch and waited. Once he knew she was home safe, he could relax, he told himself. Although he'd seen Mia leave earlier with Patti and Rowena, he didn't even want to consider the possibility that Celeste might not come home at all.

Ray blamed himself for not telling Celeste how he felt about her. He'd waited too long, proceeded too cautiously. Sitting there on the front porch, with the cool, dry desert breeze fanning his face, Ray made a promise to himself. The next time he had an opportunity, he'd tell Celeste he loved her.

Celeste returned, setting the steaming mug of hot chocolate on the place mat in front of him. When she lifted her eyes to his, they held a flicker of uncertainty. She set down her cup and took a deep breath, squaring her shoulders.

"I have a confession to make. I didn't go out with Giorgio because he sent me gift baskets. I accepted the date because of my feelings for you."

Ray shook his head. "I don't understand."

Celeste seemed to be studying the pattern on the delicate teacup she held in front of her. "I thought I was just lonely and maybe that was why I felt such a strong attraction to you. But I know now that isn't true. It's because of who you are."

"And who's that?"

A moment ago her gray eyes had been troubled. Now the gaze she turned on him was as calm as the fathomless depths of the sea. "A good, honest, decent man. The kind of man I've always hoped for. I'm ready to give us a second chance, Ray. That is, if you still want me."

The love and trust that shone from Celeste's eyes shattered the protective shell that had encased his heart for so long. He'd seen the same look the summer they dated. Then he'd felt elated, joyful, yes, even triumphant. He'd loved and conquered. Now, eight years later, he was humbled. "I'm not sure I deserve you."

She came to him. Gently, she touched his mouth with her fingertips. "Shhh."

When she replaced her fingertips with her lips the sweetness of her kiss inflamed him beyond all reason. He'd been with plenty of women in his life, beautiful, sophisticated women who were willing to do anything to please him. None of them came close to stirring the soul-deep emotion he experienced from that single kiss.

She glanced down at him, her expression shy but inviting. "Why don't we sit on the couch? It's much more comfortable."

Ray wasn't a religious man but as he followed Celeste into the living room, he offered a silent prayer. *Dear God, don't let me screw it up this time.*

Chapter Eight

As Celeste walked around the living room dimming lamps, it occurred to her that not long ago she'd made the same loop with completely different intentions. She paused at the entertainment center to light a pair of banana nut bread–scented candles.

"What's with the smile?" Ray asked.

Celeste joined him on the couch. "I was thinking about the first time you came over. I turned on every light in the house and practically shoved you out the door. You're a hard man to discourage."

"You have no idea."

The rasp of his voice still hung in the air as he took her into his arms. She didn't resist this time.

How could she? She'd been waiting so many years. Waiting for her dream lover to reappear. Only, this time he was warm and real.

She wound her arms around his neck, closed her eyes and tilted her face upward in sweet expectation.

Slowly, tenderly, his mouth possessed her. The warmth of his kiss seeped into the deepest recesses of her being, filling the spaces that had been empty for so long. The aroma of pine and juniper filled her nostrils. The scent was indescribably masculine, unmistakably Ray. It felt so right in his arms, and familiar somehow. Like coming home.

A slight groan escaped from Ray's lips as he tucked her head against his chest. She sighed and snuggled closer.

"We need to talk," he said.

Celeste blinked up at him. Talk? Of course they needed to talk. But did it have to be right now? Reluctantly, she pulled away, making an effort to straighten her shirt and smooth her hair. As she left the comfort of Ray's embrace, a cold chill passed through her. What if she was wrong and Ray didn't return her feelings? What if . . .

"I have something I need to tell you. You know, to clear the air. So we can have a fresh start," Ray said.

Celeste felt her heart tighten in her chest. She forced herself to take a deep breath and look into his eyes. She saw vulnerability there, a plea for understanding. Hadn't she just told Ray she was ready to give them another chance? Here she was, five minutes later, doubting her instincts. Old habits died hard.

Gently, she took his hand in hers. "You can tell me anything."

"It's about that night, when I first came to your house." Ray paused. "Well, I guess there's no good way to say it. Your flat tire wasn't an accident."

Celeste felt all the tension drain out of her. She broke into a grin. "I suspected as much," she said. "Ray Fontana, you are a very bad man."

Ray pulled her into his arms again. "I know," he whispered into her hair. "Do you think you can re-form me?"

Celeste traced the outlines of his scarred warrior's face with her fingertips. "I wouldn't want to."

Their lips met in a kiss of hope and forgiveness. Though they were older and wiser now, their passion burned as brightly as ever. Any hope she had for a safe, uncommitted life went up in smoke the moment she saw Ray in the hospital cafeteria.

A twinge of guilt shot through her. She'd told Ray she was ready to give them a second chance but she was withholding the single most important piece of information about their past, present, and future. Should she tell him about Mia? she wondered.

Gently, she broke free of his embrace. She needed a few minutes to think. "I'll heat up our drinks. Don't go away."

Ray looked a little surprised but recovered quickly. "I'm not going anywhere," he said.

Not going anywhere. The words echoed in her head as she put Ray's hot chocolate in the microwave.

How could she be sure of that? Ray had a life in Miami. When Gus got well enough to run the shop, Ray might go back to Florida. And if he did decide to stay in Aubrey's Landing, how could she be sure things would work out between them? Their relationship was so new. They were just getting to know each other again.

The microwave beeped and she replaced Ray's hot chocolate with her herbal tea. When she was much younger she'd made the mistake of going too far, too fast. Now she'd be risking not only her own heart, but Mia's. Mia had lost one daddy. She couldn't bear to put her daughter through that again.

Another thought occurred to her, one that caused the muscles in her neck and shoulders to tense. When Ray learned the truth, would he be able to forgive her?

"So what did you decide?" Ray asked as she returned to the living room with their cups. She felt his dark gaze penetrate her carefully arranged expression and hoped he couldn't read the emotions just beneath the surface. Ray's cup rattled against its saucer as she set them on the coffee table.

Sitting beside him on the couch, she attempted to appear nonchalant. "What do you mean?" she asked.

"I saw that little pucker between your eyes before you escaped to the kitchen. It's a dead giveaway that something's wrong. You're not backing out on me are you?"

Celeste sighed and set down her cup. "Remind me never to play poker with you."

"So . . . give me the bad news."

She searched for the right words, not daring to look Ray in the eye. "It's not bad news, really. I just think we should go slow. I mean, we're not kids anymore and I have Mia to consider. It hurt her so badly when Blake died. She's just starting to recover." Thanks in large part to Ray's attention, Celeste realized. Mia started to blossom when he moved next door.

Ray expelled a puff of breath. "Whew. Is that all? I couldn't agree more."

His expression held warmth, compassion, tenderness—everything she'd dreamed of in a man. On the rare occasions when she'd allowed herself to dream. "Really?"

Ray chuckled. "Really. As much as I'd love to be with you, I understand your desire to do things right this time. Believe me, angel, I would never intentionally hurt you or Mia. I know it will take time to regain your trust."

He held up a hand to silence Celeste's protest. "It's okay. We have some painful history. So let's go slow. God knows, I don't want to lose you again."

Looking at Ray through a prism of tears, Celeste saw the troubled adolescent and the compassionate man. At that moment, she realized she loved them both. And probably always would.

"Thank you," she said. It was all she could manage. A single tear spilled over her eyelid and rolled down her cheek.

"Come here, angel."

Celeste relaxed against Ray's chest. It felt so safe and secure there. She didn't know how long she stayed in the warm cocoon of his embrace, but she closed her eyes and wished it could last forever.

"Celeste?"

"Ummmm," she murmured.

"What happened to Mia's father?"

Celeste felt herself stiffen. She didn't talk to anyone about this, hadn't for years. But Ray deserved the truth. She took a deep breath and plunged ahead.

"He was shot."

"What?" The single word rang out with the force of a hammer blow. Reluctantly, Celeste turned to face him.

"Blake got mixed up with the wrong crowd. We were living in Phoenix at the time. He and I were having problems and he started staying away from home more and more. I found out later that he was using and selling cocaine."

"I can't believe I haven't heard about this," Ray said.

"Not many people know. Father kept it out of the newspapers. The police said it could have been a robbery, but considering Blake's lifestyle, it was more likely a drug deal gone bad. They never found his killer."

Ray gently pulled her hands apart. She hadn't realized she'd been twisting them in her lap. He engulfed one in both of his, resting it on his muscular thigh. "And you blamed yourself."

Celeste shrugged. She couldn't deny it. God knows, she'd tried to be a good wife to Blake. But she'd never really loved him. Not the way she loved Ray. She'd always wondered if maybe she'd tried a little harder, things might have been different.

Ray seemed to read her thoughts. "It's not your fault, angel. We all make choices in life. It sounds to me like Blake made some pretty poor ones."

Celeste squeezed his hand. She felt better for having told him; lighter, as if a burden had been lifted. At least she'd been able to let one secret out into the open.

"Why don't you turn around so I can rub your shoulders?"

If she couldn't be in Ray's arms, at least she'd feel his hands on her. The thought brought a warm flush to her cheeks. She'd definitely experienced more than comfort in Ray's embrace. Her eyes strayed the length of his denim-clad body. Even by candlelight, it was evident that he felt the same.

Ray caught the direction of her glance and gave her a slow, sexy grin. Hurriedly, she turned her back, trying to hide her embarrassment. She just about melted into the couch when she felt his warm breath against her neck. He nuzzled her earlobe, sending shivers down her spine.

"I never said it would be easy, angel," he whispered.

"Oh, you are a bad man."

At dawn the next morning, Ray rolled out of bed. He'd slept only a few hours but rarely remembered feeling more alive.

"Morning, Pooch. Beautiful day, isn't it?"

Although the old dog thumped his tail a couple of times, his chin remained planted firmly between his paws. He lifted accusing eyes to his owner.

Ray crossed over to rub his ears, just the way Pooch liked it. "I'm sorry, old fella. I had important things to do last night. If you come for a run with me, I'll buy you the biggest marrow bone at the Farm Fresh Market."

Whether Pooch understood "run" or "bone" or every word he said, Ray couldn't be sure, but the dog jumped up and began dancing around him in circles.

Ray laughed. "Okay, buddy. Why don't you go out in the backyard while I shower and change into my jogging shorts? I'll be ready in just a few minutes."

The stinging water felt wonderful. As he lathered his body, Ray thought about the evening he'd spent with Celeste. Everything had been perfect. Well, almost everything. A splinter of guilt pricked his conscience. He hadn't told Celeste he loved her, as he promised himself he would.

Ray turned off the shower and reached for a towel. Words didn't come easy to him. He was better at showing people how he felt. He planned to surprise Celeste with fresh fruit and croissants from the market, but that didn't exactly say "You're the woman I want to spend my life with."

He could tell her the truth about his life in Miami. Instantly, he rejected that idea. Their relationship was too new and fragile to risk jeopardizing it now. Eventually, when the time was right, Celeste and Mia would join him in Bal Harbour. They'd shop together for a bigger house and enroll Mia in the best private school. He'd give them the kind of life they deserved.

Somehow, the thought of going back to Miami made Ray's mood plummet. No need to think about that now, he told himself. First, he'd win Celeste. There'd be time for truth-telling later.

Ray wrapped a towel around his waist and hurried into the kitchen to start the coffee. He wanted to get back before Celeste woke up. The thought of her sleep-warmed body inspired thoughts that were probably illegal in Arizona on a Sunday morning.

Possibly even more satisfying than holding her in his arms was the knowledge that she had begun to let him into her confidence. She'd shared the most painful event of life with him. Now he wanted to do something for her.

On the way to the market, Ray pondered his dilemma. What would make Celeste happy? She didn't care for material things. That was one of the qualities he loved about her. After dealing with the social-climbing crowd in Miami, Celeste's warm and giving nature was as refreshing as an ocean breeze.

But that was the problem. What could he buy someone whose greatest satisfaction in life came from helping others?

Ray stopped in the middle of the sidewalk and snapped his fingers. "That's it!" he said. Why hadn't he thought of it before?

Brought up short on the leash, Pooch looked at his owner reproachfully.

"Sorry, boy." Ray began jogging again. "I just figured out what to get for Celeste."

Pooch grinned over his shoulder, but Ray's next words were directed more at himself than the dog.

"A new OB Center."

Chapter Nine

Celeste closed and locked her office door late Tuesday afternoon. Ray had invited them over for dinner that evening and she had news she was bursting to share with him.

Not even Dr. Bandini had been able to dampen her good mood. The doctor glared in response to her polite greeting when she passed him in the hospital corridor that morning. She felt a stab of guilt when she saw his swollen nose and discolored eyes, but only for a moment. Perhaps the pain and embarrassment Giorgio Bandini had experienced would make him think twice before he accosted another woman.

Over breakfast on Sunday morning, Ray admitted he'd jogged by the hospital and placed the gift baskets at her office door. She should have known, Celeste thought as she walked toward her car in the employee parking lot. Only Ray could have been so thoughtful—although she suspected he had some coaching from a couple of pint-sized matchmakers.

Celeste smiled as she slid behind the wheel. Saturday night Ray had awakened feelings she buried long ago. Then Sunday morning, well, spending time alone with Ray was like biting into a pastry and finding a delicious cream center. It just kept getting better.

If only he'd said the words she longed to hear. Celeste mentally shook herself as she pulled in front of her father's house to pick up Mia. One evening with Ray and already she was wishing for a deeper commitment. Hadn't she been the one who'd resisted getting involved? Ray was probably afraid of scaring her off. He'd shown her plainly enough how he felt. In time, he'd find the words to tell her.

Celeste peeked out the kitchen curtains and tried not to smile as Ray cremated the steaks. He looked so adorably clueless with that worried frown on his face. Far be it from her to tell him he hadn't let the coals burn down long enough.

She'd insisted on helping with dinner and had been given the job of baking potatoes and making salad. She opened the microwave door and turned the potatoes, then reset the timer. A couple more minutes ought to do it. On the counter beside the microwave a rather misshapen pumpkin waited to be carved. Halloween was Friday night and Ray had promised to help Mia make a jack-o-lantern.

Returning to the window to check Ray's progress, she saw him dance over to the ice chest with a flaming hunk of meat in his tongs. She couldn't quite make out what he was saying but imagined little x's, astericks, and exclamation points hovering over his head.

Ray grabbed a cream soda, popped the top with one hand, and doused the inferno. He stood for a long moment, contemplating the blackened remains of what had once been an expensive T-bone. The two steaks on the grill didn't look much better. The phrase "burned beyond recognition" came to mind.

Celeste let the curtains fall back into place. "Mia, honey."

Mia came from the living room where she'd been watching TV with Pooch. "Yes, Mom?"

"Run next door and get that package of hot dogs out of our refrigerator, will you?"

They dined on baked potatoes, salad, and hot dogs without the buns.

"I don't really like the breads, anyway," Mia said around a bite of hot dog smothered in ketchup.

"You did a perfect job of grilling these," Celeste offered.

Ray grinned. "Right. It's a good thing I had the steaks to practice on. At least I can promise you cookies and ice cream for dessert."

"Yay!" said Mia.

"They had special ghost-and-goblin-shaped cookies at the Farm Fresh Market," Ray said. "What are you going to be for Halloween, Mia?"

"I'm going to be Sacagawea." Mia's eyes glowed with excitement.

"The Indian maiden who guided Lewis and Clark."

Mia bobbed her head up and down. "Uh-huh, and Rowena's going to be Pocahontas."

"I think I'm beginning to see a pattern here."

"Mia and Rowena joined a Girl Guides troop at the church," Celeste explained. "In fact, according to Micah, starting the troop was their idea."

Ray looked at the two faces, watching him expectantly. He knew Celeste was concerned about Mia being too shy and reserved. Maybe joining this guide thing would help her gain confidence. In any event, it seemed to be a pretty big deal to both mother and daughter. "That's wonderful, Mia. I mean, I think it's great." Ray paused, looking from one to the other. "What exactly does a Girl Guide do?"

The girls exchanged amused glances.

"They earn patches for learning to do things like reading a compass or cooking a meal," Celeste said.

"Or telling a campfire story," Mia put in.

"It's a very nature-oriented program. The girls will participate in lots of fun outdoor activities," Celeste added.

"And, I get to wear my uniform to school, with all the patches on it." Mia patted her chest, to show where dozens of patches would decorate her uniform. She looked as proud as if she'd already earned them.

Their enthusiasm was contagious. "Wow! That sounds fantastic. When do you start?" Ray asked.

Celeste ticked off the items on her fingers. "A notice inviting girls to join was published in the paper last week. Patti has been passing the word at the rec center, and we put up posters advertising an organizational meeting for next Saturday."

Mia bounced up and down in her chair. "We're going on a canoe trip on Thanksgiving, to the Topock Gouge. We're going to see where the Indians wrote on rocks. And big horn sheep!"

Ray understood why Celeste had seemed so pleased about the Girl Guide troop. He'd never seen Mia so animated. The quiet, serious little girl, who often behaved like a miniature adult, had transformed into a squirmy, excited seven-year-old.

"It's the Topock *Gorge,* sweetie," Celeste corrected. "Although it does look like the Colorado River gouged the canyon out of solid stone."

"Is Micah going along?" Ray asked. "The river

can be dangerous if you don't have an experienced guide."

Celeste nodded. "I couldn't agree more. That's why we arranged for Bluewater Adventures to lead us. They've been taking groups through the gorge for fifteen years. They'll supply the canoes, life jackets, and a couple of experienced guides. Micah's going too. But we could still use a few more adult volunteers."

"Could *you* go, Ray?" Mia seemed to be holding her breath as she waited for an answer.

The pleading note in Mia's voice wrenched Ray's heart. Why hadn't he seen this coming? He hadn't been in the water since the boat racing accident in Paris had ended his career and almost cost him his life. Unconsciously, he rubbed the jagged scar above his left eye.

It's a canoe, for God's sake. It doesn't even have a motor. Besides, what could possibly happen on a Girl Guides field trip? Looking at the hopeful faces across from him, he knew he couldn't disappoint them.

"Sure," he said. "I'd love to." *About as much as I'd love being boiled in oil.*

Mia's anxious expression dissolved into pure, radiant joy. She jumped up and ran around the table to give Ray a hug. "I knew you'd come," she said.

Ray didn't know if he could ever deserve the confidence Mia placed in him but he was sure going to try. He rumpled her thick, dark hair. "Come on, Sacagawea," he said, his voice gruff with emotion. "Let's go carve that pumpkin."

"Wait," Celeste said. "Before we adjourn to the patio, I have some good news to share with you."

Ray and Mia turned to look at her. From her tone of voice, it was clear Celeste had something important to say.

"Mia, honey, you know all those evenings Mom came home late because she was working on the OB Center?"

"The one for poor women and their babies," Mia said.

"That's right." Celeste looked up at Ray, her eyes shining with emotion. "My good news is that we received a huge anonymous donation that will help us build the OB Center a lot sooner than anyone thought possible. We plan to break ground in the spring."

He'd been right, Ray thought with satisfaction. Nothing he could have given Celeste would have made her happier.

Hell, he felt almost as thrilled as she. He wanted to hold her in his arms, to bury his face in her sweet, herbal-scented hair but he held back. Celeste had kept her distance all evening. She wasn't ready for Mia to know they'd crossed over into a more intimate relationship and he had to respect her judgment. "That's wonderful," he said, then gave in to the irresistible urge to touch by awkwardly patting her shoulder.

Mia tugged impatiently on her mother's sleeve. "What's an a-nom-i-nus donation, Mom? And why are you going to break the ground?"

Celeste laughed and stooped to pick up her daughter. "I'm sorry, sweetie. You act so grown up that sometimes I forget you're only seven."

"Seven and a half," Mia corrected.

"Right. An anonymous donation means someone gave us lots of money but didn't tell us his name. And when you 'break ground,' that means you start building."

Mia listened intently. "So a man gave you lots of money for the OB Center but you don't know who he is?"

"A man or a woman, we don't even know which. But I think we should ask God to bless this person when we say our prayers tonight. He or she has done a good and generous thing that will make lots of people's lives better."

Mia looked puzzled. "If they're doing a good thing, why do they want to keep it a secret?"

Celeste kissed Mia's cheek. "I don't know the answer, sweetie. Maybe someday we will."

Someday, Ray thought. When the mysteries of Aubrey's Landing are revealed.

* * *

Celeste sat in a new, white wicker chair on Ray's back porch and sipped iced tea as Ray and Mia slaved over their pumpkin. The table and set of four patio chairs weren't the only new items she'd noticed tonight. Ray had purchased woven place mats and pretty jewel-toned drinking glasses. Although they'd eaten on paper plates, she suspected his cutlery was new, too—heavy stainless steel with dark rosewood handles. It was really quite attractive.

What happened to the guy who thought he could coordinate colors as long as they all belonged to the fruit and spice family? An uneasy suspicion crept into her mind. Ray admitted letting the air out of her tire. Now it appeared he'd tricked her into helping him by pretending to be a decorator's nightmare. What else had he lied about? she wondered.

Mia's voice broke through her thoughts. "Look, Mom! It's finished." She held up the jack-o-lantern.

One eye was bigger than the other and the gap-toothed grin angled down and to the left. Celeste looked from the jack-o-lantern to the flushed faces of its creators. A lock of dark hair fell across Ray's forehead. He looked almost as proud as Mia. Both seemed to be anxiously awaiting her approval.

Celeste's heart melted. "It's perfect," she said. "It'll be the best jack-o-lantern in Aubrey's Landing."

Ray grinned, his teeth dazzling against tawny,

amber skin. He held an open palm above Mia's head. "Gimme five."

Mia slapped it shyly. She'd never done a high five before, but Celeste could tell she loved it. She loved everything Ray taught her.

"Come on," Ray said, helping Mia to her feet. "Let's go in the house and find a candle. We can try him out tonight."

"Want to come, Mom?" Mia asked.

"No thanks, honey. I think I'll just sit here and digest my dinner. After all those cookies and ice cream, I feel like a big fat toad."

Mia tucked her chin into her chest and lowered her voice. "Croak, croak."

Celeste reached out to swat her daughter's rear as she skittered past, giggling. "Yeah, croak. You better get out of here or I'll sit on you."

Left alone on the patio, Celeste's thoughts again became troubled. Ray had been living next door for almost two months. But what did she know about him, really? Okay, other than what her instincts told her. She mentally listed the information she'd been able to gather.

He was a boat mechanic, for . . . Native Spirit. At least she thought that was the name of his company. He lived somewhere in the Miami area.

Had he quit his job? Or just taken a leave of absence? And what about his personal life? Was there a girlfriend waiting for him in Miami?

No. She didn't believe it. The Ray she had gotten to know wouldn't lead her on. He wouldn't break her heart again. Or Mia's.

Unless all of her instincts about him were wrong.

Celeste crossed her arms over her chest and shivered. The late October evening had suddenly grown chilly. After breakfast on Sunday morning she'd been tempted to tell Ray he was Mia's father. Thank God she hadn't given in to the impulse.

Pooch thrust a wet nose against her knee, startling her. She'd forgotten he was under the table. Absently, she reached down to stroke his head.

How would Ray have reacted? she wondered. Would he become angry? Would he make demands? She couldn't really blame him. However, she had her own priorities and first on that list was protecting Mia.

It wouldn't hurt to find out more about Ray's background, especially now that their relationship had become more intimate. She reached a decision just as Ray and Mia came back, armed with a candle and long fireplace matches.

"It's a bug repellent candle," Ray explained. "So don't be surprised if you smell Raid instead of banana nut bread." His gaze held her for a moment in a warm caress. Then he placed the jack-o-lantern on his new wicker table and put the candle inside. "Would you like to light him, Mia?"

Wide-eyed, Mia glanced at her mom for permission.

Celeste nodded. "Go ahead, sweetie. It's okay as long as there's a grownup to help."

Mia climbed onto one of the chairs. Ray handed her a lighted match and together, they poked it down until the flame touched the candle wick. The jack-o-lantern flared to life, his lopsided grin a beacon in the fall twilight.

"It's beautiful," Mia breathed.

"Beautiful," Ray agreed, but he wasn't looking at the pumpkin. His dark gaze wandered over Celeste, lingering on her hair, her eyes, her lips.

Celeste felt her skin tingle as Ray's sultry expression stirred memories of their evening together. She stood and put her arm around Mia's shoulders. "I think it's about time for my little pumpkin to get ready for bed."

"Do we have to go already?" Mia asked.

"I'm afraid so. You have school tomorrow." Celeste gave Mia's shoulder a squeeze. "But I have a good idea. Why don't we invite Ray to our *Día de los Muertos* celebration on Saturday?"

"Yeah!" Mia brightened instantly at the suggestion.

Ray cocked his head to one side. "*Día de Los Muertos,*" he repeated. "You celebrate the Day of the Dead?"

"Yes, but it's not as gruesome as it sounds. It's a Hispanic tradition to visit the graves of departed loved ones on November second, as a celebration of their lives. We go every year with Rosa."

"It's lots of fun. We sweep the graves and put fresh flowers on them. Then we tell stories and have a picnic." Mia looked at him with an eager expression.

Ray grinned and touched the tip of her nose. "I'd follow you anywhere, Sacagawea." Then he looked at Celeste. "Are you sure I won't be intruding? I don't think Rosa's ready to welcome me into the bosom of her family."

"Leave Rosa to me," said Celeste.

Ray and Pooch walked them home. She turned at the door and offered her hand, but instead of taking it, Ray gave her a quick, light kiss on the cheek.

"Thanks for coming over tonight," he said.

"Th-thank you. For dinner." Good gravy. She was stammering. Celeste put a hand to her cheek where he kissed her. She felt as if his lips had left a permanent imprint on skin.

"Me too," chimed Mia, holding up her arms.

To Mia's delight, Ray picked her up and swung her around the yard. Then he planted a noisy kiss on her forehead and set her back on the porch beside Celeste.

"Will I see you on Halloween?" he asked.

Mia nodded. "We're going to trick-or-treat with Patti and Rowena. We'll come to your house first because you're right next door."

"Do you think I'll recognize you?"

Mia appeared to think that over. "Maybe not. But I bet Pooch will!" She gave him an impish grin and followed her mom into the house.

Chapter Ten

"So, tell me about Miami," Celeste said.

Ray tried not to choke on a bite of *pan de los muertos* as the delicious All Souls' Day treat turned to sawdust in his mouth. He set the wedge of bread on a paper plate, next to a flat, round loaf topped with bone shapes and sprinkled with purple sugar.

Bread of the Dead. That's what their relationship would be if he didn't get this right.

They'd spent the morning in the Johansen family plot raking, weeding, and cleaning around the graves. After lunch, Rosa and Mia had gone to another section of the cemetery to place fresh flowers on the grave of Rosa's deceased husband. Although other families were picnicking nearby, none were close enough to hear their conversation.

Ray cast a uneasy glance at the upright grave marker towering over their heads. The inscription read: *Silas Johansen, Steamboat Captain on the Colorado River*. Despite the festive atmosphere in the cemetery that day, the whole scene gave Ray the creeps. How could he continue to hide his true identity with Celeste's ancestral spirits hovering close? Al Fontana may not have taught him much, but he had instilled a healthy respect for the dead.

Carefully, he arranged his features in a neutral expression. "What would you like to know?"

Celeste waved her hand in a vague, all-encompassing gesture. "Oh, you know, what you did in your free time, when you weren't working."

So far, he was on safe ground. "I enjoyed going to the theater and the opera. I jogged on the beach. And, I went out to eat a lot." He gave her a wry smile. "Cooking isn't one of my strong points."

Celeste smiled but she seemed uncomfortable. Had she heard something? Ray wondered. With a sense of impending doom, he waited for the next question.

"Did you go with . . . anyone special?"

So that was it. She wanted to know if he had a girlfriend in Miami. He expelled the breath he'd been holding and felt all his muscles relax. "No," he said. "There's no one special. At least, not in Miami."

He saw her expression soften. Her fingers fluttered slightly as she pushed pale hair away from her forehead.

"Come here." He patted the blanket to his right.

She knelt beside him. The expression in her blue-gray eyes reminded him of a half-wild kitten he'd adopted as a boy. She wanted to trust him but she was afraid.

"I've dated other women. Quite a few of them. But none have affected me the way you do. They don't even come close. You're one of a kind, angel."

She leaned over and kissed him softly on the lips. "Thank you," she whispered.

He ached to take her in his arms and soothe her worries away. If they were alone, he could show her how he felt. However, here in the cemetery, with kids running around and the spirits of Celeste's dead relatives watching his every move, a little self-control seemed to be in order.

He positioned himself behind Celeste and put his arms around her. With a contented sigh, she leaned back against his chest. Spirits or no, Ray felt himself responding to her closeness.

"Ray?"

He lowered his head to inhale the rain-washed freshness of her hair. "Yes, angel?"

"What exactly did you do in Miami? For work, I mean."

Caught off guard, he stiffened. Celeste sat up and looked at him.

"What's the matter?" she asked.

Ray grimaced and rubbed his calf. "I must have run too far this morning."

"You have a cramp?" Her brow furrowed with concern. "Here, let me rub it for you."

As Celeste kneaded his calf, Ray groped for an answer. This was the moment he'd been dreading. He didn't want to lie but he wasn't ready to tell the whole truth yet, either. He needed to know that Celeste loved *him.* Not the designer of the fastest offshore racing boat to ever hit the straits of Florida; not the largest stockholder and chairman of the board of Native Spirit Boats; not the philanthropist, the art collector, or the millionaire. Just Ray.

"I worked for Native Spirit Boats," he said. "First as a mechanic. Later I worked in the production and design department." His statement was basically true. He tinkered with boats, then he designed them. And he built the company from the ground up, although he wasn't ready to mention that just yet.

"As a mechanic?" Celeste raised her eyes, questioning. She continued massaging his calf muscle, slowly working up to his thigh.

Damn! She was making it very difficult for him to concentrate. Ray took a deep breath. "Sort of. I was down in the trenches, so to speak."

Celeste looked confused. "But what did you *do*?"

There was no way out. "I, uh, was involved in designing a new type of racing boat."

"Why, Ray, I think that's wonderful. Why have you been so modest? I always knew you had a gift."

Ray took Celeste's hand from his calf and pressed the palm to his lips. "You think I have a gift?"

She turned a delicious shade of pink. He was playing dirty and he knew it, but he had no desire to continue that line of questioning.

"M-mechanically speaking, I mean," she stammered.

He smiled at her, then one by one he took her fingers into the warmth of his mouth, tasting them with his lips and tongue. There were millions of nerve-endings in the fingertips, more than in almost any other part of the body. Judging from Celeste's expression, every one of those nerves was transmitting erotic impulses to her brain. Her eyes fluttered closed as her mouth formed a rosy O.

God, but she was sensitive. And to think, he'd once described her as rigid. *All elbows and raw nerves.* He looked around to make sure no one was watching, and then lightly kissed her lips. "How about in other ways?"

Celeste's eyes popped open. She slapped his shoulder. "Stop teasing me. I bet you didn't even have a charley horse."

Ray grinned. He'd better get out of here before he did something really indiscreet. Besides, he had an important visit to make. "Want to take a walk?" he asked.

Celeste hesitated. "I don't want to worry Rosa and Mia."

He pulled the daily planner from his back pocket and tore out November 2nd. "Here. Leave them a note. We won't be gone long."

Hand in hand, they strolled through the autumn sunshine, past a couple of kids tossing a football, and a family eating fried chicken on a brightly colored Mexican blanket. The main road through the cemetery had been closed to automobile traffic today. Ray headed for the flower vendor stationed beside the road.

"Which do you like?" he asked.

Celeste considered the cart full of flowers. There were orange and yellow gladiolas, white mums, and pink carnations. She was immediately drawn to a bouquet of lavender roses, set off by a spray of baby's breath and tied with a pink ribbon.

"These are lovely." She held them close to her face to catch their delicate scent, then put back on the vendor's cart. "Not very practical though. The gladiolas or mums last a lot longer."

Ray pulled a wallet from his back pocket. "I'll take the roses," he said. And then to Celeste, "They were my mother's favorite."

They walked to a newer section of the cemetery where all the gravestones were flat. Celeste recalled the groundskeeper telling her the cemetery didn't allow upright markers anymore because it was too hard to mow around them. Personally, she thought it was a shame. The old uprights had so much more personality.

Ray had become quiet. He seemed lost in his own thoughts. He'd only bought one bouquet of flowers, for his mother. She'd met Ray's mom the summer they dated. Juleska was a lovely woman, with a quiet dignity Celeste had envied.

Where was Ray's father buried? she wondered.

She didn't have to wait long to find out. In the farthest corner of the cemetery, on a low hill over-looking Parker Valley, two simple white crosses stood side-by-side under a weeping willow tree. The grave markers read Alonso Rafael Fontana and Juleska Ruth Fontana, with the dates of their birth and death.

"What a lovely spot," Celeste said. "How did you get the cemetery to agree to the crosses?"

Ray laid the bouquet of roses on his mother's grave. "We paid extra. It's what Ma wanted."

"You were close to your mother, weren't you?" Celeste asked.

Ray nodded. "Yeah. She always saw the good in people. Like you."

"How about your father?"

Ray glanced in her direction. In his dark eyes she saw surprise, followed by a flash of anger. When he spoke, his voice was as hard as the marble grave-stones. "We were happiest when he was in jail."

She was shaken by the intensity of his response. Her relationship with her father had been difficult, to say the least. She'd been furious with him, upset, disappointed, and hurt. But she'd never felt the cold disdain she heard in Ray's voice.

"There must have been some good times," she said.

He shrugged. "A few, I guess. When he was sober. You just couldn't count on him staying that way for long."

Celeste took him by the hand and led him to a shady place under the weeping willow. They sat on soft grass and looked out at the patchwork of fields in the lush valley below. "Tell me about the good times," she said.

Ray flopped down on the soft grass. He put his hands behind his head and stared up at the willow branches bending gracefully toward the ground. "My mom used to call these tickle trees when Micah and I were little. The branches tickle when you walk under them."

"I like that. I'll have to tell Mia."

Ray shot a quick, indecipherable glance in her direction, then returned his gaze to the willow tree. "Before I was born, Al wanted to give my mom a present. They didn't have much money. He was doing odd jobs, fixing cars, yard work, whatever he could to earn a buck. Mom waited tables at Betty's right up until the day she went into labor. Anyway, he made Mom the most beautiful cedar chest you've ever seen."

"He must have been a talented carpenter."

"Yeah, and a damn good auto mechanic too. Or so I hear. By the time I was old enough to under- stand anything, he was drunk most of the time."

Celeste felt saddened by Ray's hurt and anger. She knew the pain wouldn't have cut so deeply if Ray hadn't loved his father very much. Her heart ached for the little boy who had learned to protect himself by hardening his heart and denying that love. Maybe talking about his feelings would start the healing process.

"Anything else?" she prodded gently.

Ray's funny little, half-sad smile tugged at her heart. "Yeah. He taught me to whistle."

Celeste laughed, a welcome release for the emo- tions that had been building inside her. Tears stung her eyes. "So your dad gave you the ability to work with your hands and a love for music. Those are valuable gifts."

A note of bitterness crept into his voice. "Yeah, and don't forget the bad attitude and addictive per- sonality. Folks around here think I'm just like him."

"That's not true! You might have inherited some of Alonso's personality traits, but what you've done with them is entirely different." Agitated, Celeste got up and began to pace back and forth under the weeping willow. "For instance, you don't drink at all, do you?"

Ray looked up at her through half-closed lids. "No, I've always channeled my energy into other things: work, sports, whatever interested me at the time. Besides, I promised Ma I wouldn't drink. One alcoholic in the family is enough."

"Aha!" Celeste waved a hand in his direction to emphasize her point. "You see? You've done something constructive with that quality."

He grinned at her lazily. "If you say so, angel."

His nonchalant attitude further incensed her. What could she say to break through that carefully constructed wall of indifference? She plunged ahead. "And you do not have a bad attitude!"

Ray cocked his head at her. An amused and disbelieving smile pulled at his lips.

Celeste stopped pacing. She took a deep breath and dropped her hands to her sides. "Okay, sometimes you have a bad attitude," she conceded. "Like now. But whether you choose to believe it or not, you have a lot of good in you, Ray Fontana—and so did your father."

In one graceful movement, Ray rolled to his feet. He folded her in his arms, and kissed her gently on the cheek. Celeste remained stiff and unyielding. She wasn't about to be put off so easily.

"How can I argue with my greatest champion?" Ray asked. He gave her a quick, firm hug and then released her. Walking to his mother's grave, he pulled one of the lavender roses from the bouquet and placed it on Al Fontana's marker. "For the good times," he said.

Maybe it was a quirk of the dappled autumn sunlight, or maybe just wishful thinking, but for a second Celeste could have sworn Ray's expression softened a little. She sent a quick prayer heavenward that she'd witnessed the beginning of forgiveness.

All her instincts and training led to one certain conclusion: Until Ray forgave his father, he would never love or accept himself.

On the way home, Mia fell asleep with her head on Ray's shoulder. The sound of Rosa and Celeste's quiet conversation in the front seat faded to a hum as Ray leaned back and closed his eyes.

A mental picture of Celeste pacing and waving her arms flashed in his brain. He'd enjoyed her spirited defense so much, he couldn't resist exaggerating his indifference. Had anyone ever been so passionate on his behalf? He didn't think so.

In truth, he'd been touched by her confidence in him. And her unshakeable belief in the innate goodness of all mankind, including Al Fontana.

Maybe she had something there, he thought. Maybe Al was one of the reasons fate brought him back to Aubrey's Landing. He'd talk to Micah about their father, sometime soon. Judging from their conversation in Betty's Diner, his brother struggled with his own demons from the past.

Maybe between the two of them, they could lay some ghosts to rest.

Ray shifted Mia's small, warm body into his arms and followed Celeste into the house. Dr. Nilson's house. Even after all these years, he felt like an infidel breaching the inner sanctum as he walked through the imposing double doors.

Inside, he settled Mia on the living room sofa, then joined the women in the kitchen. Rosa stood at the stove, stirring something in a big pot.

"What's that wonderful smell?" he asked.

Rosa pretended not to hear him but her stiff posture telegraphed disapproval. All morning she'd avoided him whenever possible.

At least she hadn't crossed herself and run away. He'd take that as progress.

"It's Mexican hot chocolate, flavored with cinnamon and almonds. Rosa makes the best." Celeste stood and pushed her chair under the table. "If you don't mind, I need to go up and say hello to my father. You and Rosa can visit while I'm gone." She glanced at Rosa's back and then grinned at him mischievously. "After all, this is a day for reconciliation."

"In that case, I'll go with you."

"What?" Celeste looked at him as if he'd lost his mind. Even Rosa forgot her animosity and turned to stare.

Ray stood. "I've given it a lot of thought. If we're going to see each other, we need to be upfront about it. I want to let your father know that my intentions are honorable."

Rosa spoke first. "Dr. Nilson, he's not going to like it."

Ray turned and met her gaze. "Maybe not. But at least we'll have done the right thing." He turned to Celeste. "What do you say, angel?"

Celeste hesitated for a moment, then drew herself up a little straighter. "You're right. I'll have to tell him sooner or later. Are you sure you want to come with me, though? It's not going to be pleasant."

"I'm sure."

"Rosa, would you call father on the intercom and let him know we're coming up?"

"*Sí.* I'll tell him." Rosa mumbled something unintelligible, made a sign of the cross and headed for phone.

Ray took Celeste's hand as they walked up the stairs. "It may not be as bad as you think."

Celeste shot him a quick glance. "Don't count on it."

They paused at the top. To the left, an ornate, mahogany-paneled elevator stood open, as if inviting them to enter.

"Does your father come downstairs sometimes?" Ray asked in a low voice. The dark paneling and plush, wine-colored carpet gave the upstairs a somber feeling. *Like a mortuary,* he thought.

Celeste shook her head. "We hoped he would. That's why we had the elevator installed. Since the stroke, Father's never completely regained the use of his left side. He refuses to go out in public in a wheelchair. In fact, he rarely leaves his suite of rooms."

"Is he all right . . . mentally?"

"He's as sharp as he is manipulative. Father controls half of what goes on in Aubrey's Landing from these rooms. He's not someone you want as an enemy." She turned troubled blue-gray eyes on him.

"Hey, I come in peace." He pulled a blue bandanna from his back pocket and waved it at her, hoping to break the tension. "Oops, wrong color. Should we go downstairs and borrow one of Rosa's dishtowels?"

Celeste relaxed a little. "I'm sorry. I don't mean to be so melodramatic. I just have a bad feeling about this."

"Don't worry about me, angel. I can take care of myself." He squeezed her hand. "Come on. Let's get it over with."

To their right, three closed doors faced the long, open landing. He could tell the upstairs had been remodeled to accommodate Dr. Nilson's wheelchair. Celeste stopped at the middle door and knocked.

"The lady or the tiger?" whispered Ray.

Celeste rolled her eyes at him, took a deep breath and let it out slowly. "Definitely the tiger." She pushed the door open.

Massive. The word popped into his brain, followed immediately by *intimidating* and *regal.* The decorator must have been instructed to spare no expense in making Dr. Nilson feel like the emperor of his own private universe.

A king-size bed with a heavy mahogany headboard dominated the room. The blue and gold spread was turned down to reveal wine-colored sheets and pillowcases. Ray noticed an indentation in the center of the bed and several pieces of paper scattered about. The doctor had evidently been reading when he received the heads-up from Rosa.

An executive desk occupied the right-hand corner of the bedroom. Financial magazines, medical journals, and today's *Wall Street Journal* were stacked neatly on top. A couple of solid, upholstered mahogany chairs faced a low glass-topped table. Behind the seating arrangement, a picture window looked out at the pool and courtyard below. In another home, this might have been called a conversation center. Here, he had the feeling *inquisition* would be more appropriate.

Dark, original oil paintings hung in ornate golden frames on the blue silk wallpaper. Ray thought he recognized a Renoir.

"Pretty impressive," he said. "Where's your father?"

Celeste sighed. "He must be in the war room. It's where he conducts all his business." She knocked at another heavy wooden door between the desk and picture window.

"Come in."

The words were very slightly slurred. As Celeste opened the door, Ray felt he was entering another world. Where the furnishings in the bedroom had been opulent and formal, the war room was definitely high tech. The latest and most expensive computer and laser printer, a fax machine, color copier, and a drafting table with not one, not two, but three telephones filled the dimly lit interior. In the center of all this gadgetry sat Dr. Leander Nilson.

The doctor turned his wheelchair to face them as they entered the room. He held two steel balls in his left hand, which he rolled through his fingers, although his arm remained immobile on the black silk of his dressing gown. He reminded Ray of a malevolent spider, waiting patiently for his prey.

"Celeste." The single word was a greeting, a question, a command.

Ray instinctively took Celeste's hand. *Courage.* He sent the word to her with all the force his brain could muster and felt a reassuring squeeze in return.

"Father, you remember Ray Fontana."

"I remember." The words were as cold as the

doctors icy blue eyes and snow-white hair. As cold as the blue field on the computer and the gun-metal gray tabletop. The room temperature, already chilly, seemed to drop several degrees.

At that moment, Ray sensed the truth. He'd faced down an auditorium full of angry stockholders, sent competitors to their knees, but never had he confronted a more implacable enemy. He steeled himself for the confrontation.

"Hello, Dr. Nilson," he said. "I've come to tell you that I'm dating Celeste. I know you didn't approve of me in the past, but I hope to show you that I've changed. That I can be worthy of your daughter."

All the old feelings came rushing back. He was twenty-five years old again, facing Dr. Nilson at the front door. *She's gone to college now. Back to her real life. You don't belong in that world.*

Ray felt himself break out in a cold sweat. The past and present oozed together, like the colors in a grotesque cubist painting.

"You'll never be worthy of Celeste."

If you love her, leave now and don't ever come back, Ray heard the words from the past echo through his brain.

"You're wrong, Father." Celeste's words rang out, strong and true.

In the dim light, Ray saw blue sparks glint in her eyes. Fire and ice, he thought. She's a match for her father. She just doesn't know it yet.

"Ray is a kind, decent, and honorable man. I'm sorry you can't see that."

Leander Nilson turned his gaze on his only daughter. "I'm disappointed in you, Celeste. Gravely disappointed. If you have no pride in yourself, you could at least consider your daughter."

Celeste looked at though she'd been slapped. The old man knew exactly how to twist the dagger in her most vulnerable spot. "You're not being fair. Mia adores Ray. And you don't even know him."

Those cold, malignant eyes flicked over Ray once more, regarding him as if he were a noxious insect. Then Dr. Nilson turned to his computer. "Good night, Celeste."

They were dismissed.

Outside, Celeste clenched her fists. "How does he always do that do me?" she asked.

"What's that, angel?" Ray had followed her onto the landing.

"Put me at a disadvantage. Make me feel guilty, even though I know I've done nothing wrong."

"He's had years of practice." He turned her to face him. "For what it's worth, I thought you were magnificent. Thank you."

In the warmth of Ray's approving gaze Celeste felt herself begin to relax. "Really?"

He gave her a slow, sexy smile and then took her into his arms. "Really."

Celeste held perfectly still, letting the strength in

his hard, fighter's body flow through her. As always, she felt shaken by the confrontation with her father. But this time, things had been different. This time, she'd had someone there to support her.

Reluctantly, Celeste pulled away. "We better go downstairs and reassure Rosa. She's probably wondering if we made it out alive."

As they walked down the wide mahogany staircase, she turned to Ray one last time. "Any regrets?" she asked.

Ray shook his head. "I'd go to hell and back for you, angel."

Celeste hoped her father wouldn't make that necessary.

Dr. Nilson glanced impatiently at his watch before turning back to the computer screen. He'd been attempting to compose a letter to an old friend and business associate in Phoenix but found he couldn't concentrate. The redevelopment of downtown Aubrey's Landing seemed much less important after his daughter's visit that afternoon.

It wasn't like him to let the situation get this far out of control. If he'd only been paying attention, perhaps he could have nipped their relationship in the bud. Celeste was much too trusting, just like her mother.

Leander's eyes misted over as he thought of his wife. Alice had been the best wife any man could want—sweet, gentle, and so eager to please. She'd died trying to give him a son.

If only he'd realized how much he loved her, he may have been able to stop her. It was the only time she'd disobeyed him. She said she hoped a son would cement their marriage, make him forget about . . .

Leander Nilson shook his head, trying to dislodge the painful memories. He felt like an old man tonight, full of regrets. All his physician's skill hadn't been able to save Alice, but it wasn't too late for Celeste.

"Where is that damn woman?" He pushed a button on the arm of his motorized wheelchair and rolled smoothly out of the war room.

"You looking for me, Doc?" Sheila McCloud slouched in the doorway leading to his suite of rooms. She looked even more slovenly than usual, her red hair wild and uncombed under a perky white nurse's cap. The rest of her outfit, high-heeled black sandals, form-fitting knit top and tight denim pants would have been more appropriate at the neighborhood bar.

That was probably where she'd come from, Leander thought with distaste. Although he abhorred Sheila McCloud personally, he'd come to have great respect for her ability as an informant. She'd once held a private investigator's license in another state, but had it pulled for attempting to bribe a city official. The woman could worm information out of anyone, from police officers to petty criminals.

"You're a mess, McCloud. Go comb your hair. And take off that ridiculous cap."

The woman gave him an insolent smile as she strolled past him into the adjoining bathroom. "My, aren't we grumpy tonight. What's got you in such an uproar?"

Leander gritted his teeth, trying to ignore her impertinence. "I have a job for you. An important job that will pay well."

Sheila McCloud stopped combing. "Oh?"

"I want you to investigate someone for me. You'll need to travel to Miami, and spend a week or two there, possibly longer. Of course, I'll pay for the airline tickets and all your expenses." And of course, she'd pad her expense account.

McCloud came out of the bathroom. She'd pulled her hair back in a ponytail and removed the nurse's cap. "Who's the lucky guy?"

"Raymond Fontana."

The buxom redhead flopped down in a chair. "And what exactly am I looking for? If you don't mind me asking."

Leander thought for a long moment before answering. Ever since she'd been a child, Celeste had championed the less fortunate. That trait led her to choose a career in social services, and no doubt explained her attraction to Ray Fontana.

Once, he'd been able to protect her from Fontana. This time, he had the feeling it would be much more difficult. He fixed McCloud with a steely gaze.

"Bring me something unforgivable."

Chapter Eleven

The canoe sliced through the cold, deep water of Topock Gorge. Ray mechanically dipped his paddle into the swiftly moving river, hoping he didn't look as nervous as he felt.

Hell, nervous didn't even begin to cover it. Scared spitless would be more accurate. He'd escaped death once on the Seine River in Paris and had sworn he'd never set foot in a boat again.

As if to confirm his forebodings, the party of canoes entered the narrowest portion of the gorge, aptly named Devil's Elbow, where sheer rock walls rose on either side of the Colorado River. The water changed from a bright sparkling blue to dark emerald green as they glided silently through the shadowed canyon.

173

Micah turned around in the canoe ahead of them. "How you doing back there?" he called.

Ray nodded and gave him the thumbs-up sign. Behind him, he heard Celeste and Mia respond with an enthusiastic "Great!"

Micah, Patti, and Rowena led the covey of six canoes through the narrow gorge. So far, the Girl Guides' first field trip had been a resounding success. They'd seen several wild burros, and as they passed by the Needles Mountain wilderness, a majestic big horn sheep.

Best of all, no one had fallen in the river. Yet.

Ray made sure all the girls were securely fastened into their life jackets. He and Micah checked and double-checked the vests supplied by Bluewater Adventures. In addition, each girl had brought a change of clothes, just in case someone fell in.

Not on my watch, Ray thought. The one bright spot of this expedition was the fact that it was too late in the year to go swimming.

"That's Mojave Rock, on the left," Micah called, pointing to a red monolith that jutted out into the river. "We'll stop there for lunch."

Ray relayed the information to Celeste and Mia and they all began to paddle toward the Arizona side of the river. Behind them, the other canoes followed suit.

As they drew closer to the rock cliffs, Ray saw the beach formed by this natural inlet. He'd been here before, of course, in his younger days. There probably wasn't an inch of the Colorado River between Needles and Parker he hadn't explored, either on foot or behind the wheel of a boat. But those days were long gone.

They hit the beach with a whoosh, and Ray jumped out to pull the canoe onto the sand. The ground had never felt so good beneath his feet. For the first time since they left Topock that morning he began to relax.

He lifted Mia out of the canoe. "So, Sacagawea, how did you like the ride?"

"Cool."

The ultimate compliment, for a seven-year-old. Mia's eyes sparkled with excitement. At that moment, Ray knew nothing could have prevented him from sharing this adventure with Mia. *Not even an exaggerated, although not entirely unreasonable, fear of drowning.* He turned to offer a hand to Celeste but she'd already climbed out of the canoe.

"Wow! That water's cold."

"Sixty-two degrees, year round." Ray tilted his head to one side as he regarded her, standing ankle-deep in the river. Her eyes reflected the hues of the water and her blond hair shone like a halo in the sunlight. She wore a smile as broad as any seven-year-old's.

"What?" She tugged at her shirt, then raked

long, slim fingers through her hair. "Why are you looking at me like that?"

"I was thinking how beautiful you look. With wild hair and a big grin on your face. The outdoors agrees with you."

Celeste waded to shore. "Thanks, I think. I'm glad to see a smile on your face too. You haven't said more than five words all morning."

"That's because I was busy paddling. I take my job as helmsman of this canoe seriously."

"Uh-huh. If you were any more serious, I'd think you might break in two. I've been watching your back all morning, and I recognize rigid posture when I see it. What gives, Fontana?"

She stood squarely in front him, hands on her hips and a determined look in her eye. The steely gaze reminded him of Dr. Nilson, only not so cold. Celeste could never be that unfeeling.

"Okay, you got me. I was a little nervous about getting into a boat. I haven't been on the water since the accident that ended my racing career. And left me with this." He gestured toward the pale lightning bolt over his left eye.

As Ray watched, her expression changed from challenging to concerned. God, but she was sweet. She touched his arm, as lightly as a kiss. "Do you want to talk about it?"

It was all he could do to keep from crushing her against him. Her caring, compassionate nature touched him more deeply than words could express. He experienced a strange catch in his throat when he tried to speak. "It's all right, angel. It was a long time ago."

Celeste looked unconvinced. "Are you sure? Sometimes talking about a fear can take away its power."

"I'll tell you all about it later. Right now, I think Micah could use a little help."

They turned to see Micah setting up a hibachi at the base of a boulder-strewn cliff. Patti and several of the moms were spreading blankets on the sand and unpacking picnic baskets. A flock of Girl Guides ran past them.

"Fine. Go help your brother. But I'm holding you to that promise, just as soon as we're alone together."

Ray cast a last admiring glance over his shoulder as he walked toward Micah. "I'll look forward to it."

"Okay, girls. What's the first rule of safe hiking?" Micah asked.

The Girl Guides wiggled and squirmed with excitement. Several jumped up and down as they chorused, "Stay with your buddy."

Ray stood behind the girls. He motioned discreetly, trying to catch his brother's attention.

"What's the second rule?" Micah asked.

"If you get into trouble, yell for a grown-up," the girls shouted.

Micah nodded. "Very good. Each pair of girls will have a grown-up in front and behind them. So don't be afraid to ask for help. Are we ready to go?"

"Yeah!" the girls screamed.

Ray waved both arms at Micah.

"Okay, everybody get with your buddy. Let's do this just the way we practiced it. Patti, lead the way."

Micah ambled over, looking as if he didn't have a worry in the world.

"Are you sure this is safe, Micah? Mia's only seven and Rowena's not much older." Ray knew he sounded like an overanxious parent, but he couldn't help himself.

Micah's kind blue eyes held the barest hint of humor. He put a big hand on Ray's shoulder. "Relax, brother. We've been preparing for this hike for weeks. Although Mia and Rowena are among the youngest girls, they're also the most agile. You can take my place if it will make you feel better."

No, damn it, it wouldn't. Micah was the most experienced hiker in the group, with the possible exception of their guide. Besides, someone had to stay with the canoes and he hadn't wanted to deprive the parent chaperones of the chance to share in the adventure.

"You go ahead," Ray said.

He stood on the sand and watched as the last of the hikers disappeared from sight. Soon they'd reach the most dangerous part of the trail. Although the climb wasn't difficult, it passed directly over a steep drop-off to the Colorado River. The guide had assured Ray he'd taken younger children than Mia on this hike. "We haven't lost anyone yet," he said.

Ray hoped Bluewater's safety record held for one more day.

He sat down on the sand, willing his tight muscles to relax. The water lapped at his bare toes as a sheriff's patrol boat sped down river. It was one of the few boats he'd seen that day. Between Memorial Day and Labor Day, water craft jammed the Colorado River, but on this mild Thanksgiving, they'd left the gorge to its native inhabitants.

He watched a snowy egret glide low over the river, in search of a midday snack. Somewhere in the shallows a fish hit the water with a plop. The scent of damp arrow weed filled his nostrils as he turned his face toward the warm November sun.

Not so many years ago, his ancestors had hiked this canyon. The Chemehueve and Paiute Indians had hunted and fished in Topock Gorge for countless generations before the white man arrived. They'd left a record of their passing etched in these rocks.

Ray felt the hairs on the back of his neck stand up. The feeling of apprehension that had weighed on him all morning intensified. It charged the air, like the last few moments before a thunderstorm. Every nerve-ending in his body tensed.

Then he heard it. A splash, followed by a loud scream.

Ray leaped to his feet. Within seconds he stood at the nearest canoe, two life jackets in hand, straining to see a human figure carried around Mojave Rock by the swiftly moving current.

"Ray! Help me!"

Mia. Somehow, he'd known it was her. Without another thought, Ray jumped into the cold water.

"Hang on, baby. I'm coming." Using the life jackets as a float he angled toward a spot downriver. Mia seemed to be holding her own, keeping her head above water. If he'd calculated right, he should reach her before the current swept her beyond his grasp.

Ray put down his head and kicked. He was close to her now, so close. No more than six feet of water separated them. He saw a look of terror on Mia's face as she reached out to him. Then, she disappeared beneath the unforgiving river.

For a moment, Ray's heart seemed to stop. The breath caught in his lungs. Fear paralyzed him. He'd cheated death on the Seine. Now the Colorado would take its revenge.

Not today, he thought. *And not Mia.*

With every ounce of his strength, he kicked toward the spot where Mia had disappeared. The current bore him in its cold embrace as he searched the river's murky depths.

She surfaced, not more than an arm's length away. Although every instinct told him to grab her, Ray restrained himself. He couldn't risk losing both vests. He held out a life jacket and spoke in a low, commanding voice.

"Take it, Mia."

Choking and coughing, the little girl grasped the jacket tightly to her chest.

Ray paddled alongside her. Finally, he could take her in his arms. Keeping a firm grasp on Mia and both jackets, he let the child cling to him until her sobs and hiccups had subsided. In truth, he needed the reassurance of holding her close, knowing she was safe. "Are you hurt, sweetheart?" he asked.

She shook her head. "No, but I'm c-c-cold."

With the shock of her fall and the cold water, he couldn't rule out hypothermia, even on a such a mild day. He'd have to get her warm and dry as quickly as possible. "Don't worry, princess. I'll have you onshore before you can sing 'I'm a Little Teapot.'"

Where had that come from? he wondered. No matter. It seemed to calm her. Grasping Mia and her life jacket firmly under one arm, he kicked toward the Arizona side of the river. To his left, the fluted bluffs rose above the water. With a little luck, he'd make land by Blankenship Bend.

"I finished the teapot song. I sang it in my head because my lips are froze," Mia said.

Ray hugged the child a little closer, trying to impart some body heat. Not that he had much to give. "Do you know any other songs?"

Mia thought for a moment. "We learned 'America the Beautiful' for Thanksgiving."

Perfect. A nice long song. He hoped she knew all the verses. Maybe it would keep her mind off being cold and frightened. "Why don't you sing that?"

Mia hummed as Ray closed the distance to shore.

"The sheriff's patrol boat reached them about the same time we did." Micah recounted the story to the concerned parents and wide-eyed Girl Guides. "Thank goodness our guide had an outboard motor in his canoe, and a radio to call for help."

"We try to be ready for any emergency," the guide said.

Celeste barely listened to Micah's explanation. She held tightly to Mia, unwilling to let her go, even though the little girl was beginning to fidget. Dressed in dry clothes and wrapped in a warm blanket, Mia seemed the none the worse for her ordeal.

She couldn't say the same for Ray. He sat slightly apart from the group that clustered around the small party of rescuers, working the knots out of the mooring line attached to one of the canoes. His complexion, several shades lighter than normal, had a greenish undertone that reminded Celeste of key lime pie.

She felt a small, impatient tug on her hand.

"Mom, I need to talk to Rowena."

Celeste followed her daughter's gaze to Rowena, who stood on the edge of the crowd gathered around Micah and the sheriff. As they watched, a fat tear rolled down Rowena's cheek and plopped onto her shirt.

Celeste squeezed her daughter's hand. "I'll go with you."

Mia put an arm around her friend. "It wasn't your fault," she whispered.

No sooner were the words out of her mouth than someone asked, "How did Mia fall in?"

All eyes turned toward the two girls. As Celeste watched, Mia stepped slightly in front of her friend, as if protecting her. She lifted her chin and said in a small, clear voice, "I heard a splash. I looked over the edge to see what it was and I lost my balance."

"We picked them up just north of Blankenship Bay," the deputy said.

The attention of the crowd swung back to the front. No one noticed the relief and gratitude that radiated from Rowena. No one but Celeste. She pulled the girls aside, then knelt in the sand beside them.

"All right, you two. Now tell me what really happened." Seeing the apprehensive looks on their faces, she added, "Don't worry. I won't be angry."

"It was pretty much like I said," Mia began. "We heard a splash and we were looking over the edge to see what made it. A big white bird flew by. Rowena turned around to look at it."

"And I hit Mia with my backpack," Rowena finished.

"That's when I lost my balance and fell in." Mia turned toward her friend. "But it wasn't your fault. I was standing too close to the edge."

Celeste hugged both girls. "Of course it wasn't your fault, Rowena. It wasn't anyone's fault. It was just an accident."

As with most accidents, the chain of events leading up to it couldn't have been predicted or prevented. Celeste had stopped to help one of the other girls, who got a piece of cactus stuck in her tennis shoe. When Mia fell in, Celeste ran to the overlook. She'd tried to jump in after Mia but Micah restrained her. It was too dangerous, he said. "Ray will get her."

And he had. She owed Ray more than she could ever hope to repay. He'd saved her daughter.

Their daughter.

Maybe the time had come to tell the truth. Ray obviously loved Mia. And he'd been so good for both of them.

Celeste shook her head. She couldn't make a life-altering decision right now. She was too shaken by the events of the day, her emotions in turmoil.

She'd invite Ray to come over tonight, after Mia went to sleep. Maybe she'd tell him then, when her mind was clearer. For now, a heartfelt thank-you was all she could manage.

Celeste stood. "We'll be leaving in just a few minutes," she said. "The sheriff's going to give us a ride home, Mia."

"Me too?" asked Rowena.

"I don't see why not. Let me ask your mom. I think she and Micah can manage the canoe on their own."

She left the girls jumping up and down with delight at the prospect of a ride in the sheriff's patrol boat. As she approached Ray, she noticed that his hands trembled at the mooring rope. A sheen of sweat covered his forehead and upper lip. When he looked at her, his gaze appeared unfocused, like someone awakening from a nightmare.

"Is it time to go?" Ray jumped to his feet, took one step and pitched forward into the sand.

"I can't swim."

Ray reclined on her living room sofa looking as relaxed as a big cat. His face had regained its normal bronzed hue and a smile curled his sensual lips.

Celeste stopped in her tracks. She'd just tucked Mia into bed for the night and was headed for the washing machine with a plastic bag full of wet clothes. "You're joking, right?"

Ray shook his head.

She sifted rapidly through her memories trying to find a missing piece. It clicked into place. "That day at Johansen Park, you said you swam across the river with your dog."

In the dim light, Ray's eyes gleamed like black obsidian. "I said that Beauty swam. I held on to her tail. I had more trust in that dog than most people I've known."

"But all those years when you were racing boats . . ."

"I liked the speed, the challenge of competing with other drivers. When you're racing, the water tells you everything you need to know. I could read it, like you read a novel. I never needed to swim, until that day in Paris."

Celeste sank into Grandmother Johansen's rocking chair, the wet clothes forgotten. "What happened?"

"I'd just passed the Statue of Liberty in the Seine River. It was toward the end of the fuel load and the boat was flying. I don't know what happened but it hit up, bounced, and then it nosedived. I was running about eighty. The whole front of the nose piece came loose and went over the top of me. There was water all around. I was fighting and kicking but I couldn't get out. That's the last thing I remember."

Celeste let out the breath she'd been holding. "But, you're here. Someone must have rescued you."

A half-smile twisted his lips. "Yeah. I think Someone did. I woke up thirty or forty feet from the boat. My life jacket had me floating. The other race boats were screaming by, missing me by inches. A patrol boat picked me up."

Celeste got up and walked to the sofa. Ray moved his legs to make room for her, then slipped an arm around her shoulders. She took his hand in both of hers. "Were you badly hurt?" she asked.

He shrugged. "A few bumps and bruises and a mild concussion."

She traced the jagged scar over his left eye with her fingertips. "And this?"

"When the boat nosedived, the front fairing came back and hit me in the forehead. It left me with an ugly scar."

Celeste snuggled closer. "I like it. It gives you character." She put her head on Ray's shoulder and inhaled his clean, woodsy scent, enjoying the comforting feel of his arm around her shoulders.

"I never raced again," Ray said. "I figured one miracle was more than I deserved. I wasn't going to press my luck."

She raised her head to look at him. "Until today. You risked your life to save Mia."

His arm tightened around her shoulder. When he

spoke, his voice was rough with emotion. "You and Mia are my life."

It's now or never, Celeste thought. No matter how angry or upset Ray became, he deserved to know the truth. She sat up straight on the couch, squared her shoulders and faced him.

"I have something to tell you," she said.

Ray leveled a steady gaze at her, his expression indecipherable. "I'm listening."

Would he be able to forgive her for keeping his daughter from him? Ray had earned her trust and confidence, as well as her love. She only hoped it wasn't too late. She took a deep breath and blurted it out.

"Mia is your daughter."

For one interminable moment, Ray said nothing. His dark eyes bored into her but she refused to look away. She'd done him a grave injustice. She knew that. She was ready to face the consequences.

Ray's face relaxed into an expression of tenderness. He reached for her, pulling her close and covering her cheeks, forehead, and hair with kisses. "I was beginning to think you'd never tell me."

Celeste couldn't get her bearings. Why was he kissing her? She'd been prepared for anger, disappointment, hurt, but not this. And what was that he'd said? Suddenly Ray's words penetrated her confusion. She pulled away from him.

"You knew?"

He nodded. "The first time I saw Mia in the hospital cafeteria, I felt something. A tug of recognition. Later, when I saw how protective you were, I sensed you might have a reason to fear me. Or at least, fear my presence in Aubrey's Landing. So I checked the baptismal records in Micah's office. Mia's birth date told me all I needed to know."

"But it could have been someone else. Or even Blake. We married in November." She would have said more but Ray gently pressed his fingers to her lips.

"I *knew*," he said. "Just like I knew I had to have you in my life. You're what's been missing all these years. When I'm with you, I feel complete. I didn't need proof that Mia was my daughter. My heart told me."

Celeste gaped at him, still unable to grasp all he was saying. "But you snooped."

Ray grinned, the old devilish grin that had so infuriated her when he'd first returned to Aubrey's Landing. "I guess my brain needed confirmation."

She slugged him in the shoulder and then threw her arms around him and hugged him fiercely. Ray returned her embrace, stroking her back, pressing warm kisses into her hair. "Angel?" he whispered.

Celeste tightened her hold, never again wanting to risk losing him again. "Yes?"

"I can't breathe."

Immediately, she let go. "Sorry. Are you sure you're not angry with me?"

Ray shook his head. The light from the hallway threw his face into relief, accentuating the planes and angles. "You reminded me of a mother bear protecting her cub. I knew I had to earn your trust. It's a gift I won't take lightly."

Gratitude filled her as she nestled against Ray's chest. She felt like she had as a young child, snug in her bed at night, listening to Rosa sing a Spanish lullaby. *Loved and protected.*

"It was an arranged marriage," she said. "I know that sounds strange in this day and age but when I told Father I was pregnant, he found me a husband. Blake seemed nice enough. He was a salesman for one of the big drug companies. He was kind to me at first and I know he truly loved Mia. I probably never should have married him but . . ."

"But you were young and frightened and alone," Ray finished for her. "I'm so sorry, angel."

Ray's mouth discovered a sensitive spot beneath her ear, and the warm glow that enveloped them became a red hot ember, tantalizing but perilous. Gently, Celeste disengaged herself. "I think I better check on Mia."

Ray's teeth gleamed in the dim light, giving him a fierce appearance. In one fluid movement, he was on his feet. He paused long enough to give her one last heart-stopping kiss. "See you tomorrow, angel."

Does a puma become a house cat? Rosa's words sounded in her brain as she closed the front door. An icy tendril of fear wrapped around her heart.

Impatient, Celeste shook it off. For God's sake, what more could the man do to prove himself? Her lack of trust had almost ruined their relationship. She wouldn't make that mistake again. From now on, her faith would be complete.

Ray tossed in his bed, replaying the events of the day. Soon, if all went well, he'd achieve his greatest desire.

He'd waited a long time for Celeste. Waited for her love, trust, and forgiveness. Hell, it seemed like he'd been waiting all his life.

He'd loved her from the first moment he saw her, singing in the choir loft. And not just for her beauty. Celeste had a sweetness about her, a radiance that intensified after he got to know her. He'd never met anyone who believed so strongly in people, or who cared so much. Even about a boy from the wrong side of the tracks.

He'd ask her to marry him tomorrow, at their belated Thanksgiving dinner. Micah would be there, along with Patti, Rowena, Rosa, and Mia. The only person missing from the family group would be Celeste's father. Although the dinner was to be held at Dr. Nilson's house, the old spider always slept through the afternoon.

Probably resting up from a night of blood sucking. No matter, Dr. Nilson couldn't ruin his plans this time. Celeste was a mature woman, capable of making her own choices. Soon, Ray hoped to provide her and Mia with the kind of life they deserved.

If she said yes.

Doubt caught him with a left hook. Was he really playing fair? he wondered. Celeste had told him the truth. Maybe he should do the same. Set all the spirits free.

Ray flexed his fingers, trying to release some of the tension building inside him. He thought longingly of the punching bag in the garage, but didn't want to wake Celeste.

Yeah, he probably ought to level with her. But he couldn't, not yet. He needed Celeste to accept his proposal with no frills, no success, no fortune attached. Then he'd know she truly loved him.

If things worked out as planned, he'd have the rest of their lives to make it up to her.

Chapter Twelve

The door opened before he had a chance to knock. Putting a finger to her lips, Celeste took Ray's hand to pull him into the house. Her soft auburn sweater hugged every curve and an apron accentuated her slender waist. Without a word, she led him to the center of the foyer, threw her arms around him and gave him an energetic kiss.

"That's some welcome, angel," Ray said.

Celeste pointed upward, where a sprig of mistletoe hung from the cathedral ceiling. "I wanted to be the first to wish you a Merry Christmas. Even though it is only the day after Thanksgiving."

"In that case . . ." Ray kissed her again, gently, tenderly, teasing her lips open with his tongue, "let me be the first to wish you a Happy New Year."

Celeste smiled at him. She seemed different this morning, more relaxed and sure of herself. Her soft, chin-length blond hair framed a face so radiant it made him weak in the knees. What had happened to the brittle, uptight woman he'd seen that first morning in the hospital cafeteria?

As if in answer to his question, Celeste leaned close to whisper in his ear, "I love you."

Ray experienced a moment of sheer panic. This wasn't the way he'd planned it. He wanted to say he loved her too but somehow the words stuck in his throat.

Celeste's eyes met his, and in that brief moment he read understanding and acceptance. She knew him, better than anyone on the planet. She knew his fears and defects, and she loved him still. He was humbled by her generosity.

"I have to go help Rosa. Father's upstairs with the night nurse. She's filling in today, just in case he needs anything. Why don't you join the others in the living room?" She turned and blew him a kiss, then disappeared into the kitchen.

Ray stood under the mistletoe, turning the ring box over in his pocket, and feeling like a complete idiot.

What was wrong with him? He loved Celeste, had loved her for as long as he could remember. So why couldn't he say the words?

He'd always had a hard time expressing his feelings. For many years he'd shown love and affection with money. He'd lavished gifts on his girlfriends, financed the Day Care Center for Micah's church, and contributed to the OB Center because he knew it would make Celeste happy.

Ray shook his head in disgust. Some tough guy. He was so afraid of intimacy he'd rather throw money at people than let them get close. All that was going to change, he vowed. Starting today.

A cozy domestic scene greeted him as he stood in the living room doorway. Patti and Micah played Scrabble on the big square coffee table in front of the fireplace. Mia and Rowena occupied a corner of the room next to the picture window facing the street. Although they pretended to play with their dolls, the girls seemed much more interested in watching the grown-ups. A crackling fire cast a warm, golden glow over the group.

Could he ever really belong here? Ray the loner, the driven man, the ruthless competitor. He wasn't sure he fit into this picture of domestic bliss.

As he hesitated in the doorway, the girls spotted him. "Ray!" they shouted. They launched themselves at him, nearly knocking him over. Each took a hand and hauled him into the room.

Micah unfolded his long legs from under the coffee table, while Patti hopped up. Both gave him welcoming hugs. Whether he deserved it or not,

Ray realized he'd become a part of all their lives. He glanced at Mia, who looked back at him with shining eyes and a somewhat smug grin.

Ray's resolve strengthened. By the end of this day, he and Celeste would be engaged. He'd tell her the truth about his life in Miami and they'd become a real family. No more ghosts, no more deception.

"Would you like to join us, brother?" Micah gestured toward the Scrabble board. "Patti is beating me mercilessly and I could use some moral support."

"Oh yeah? Who just spelled a forty-eight-point word?" Patti pointed to the board. "Xylon. He claims it's the material Superman's cape is made from."

Ray chuckled. "I learned not to play Scrabble with this guy when I was about eight. He has, shall we say, a creative command of the language."

"Aha!" Patti said. "I challenge."

"I need the girls to help me carry some things in from the car. If that's okay." Ray glanced at Patti, who was thumbing through a thick Scrabble Player's Dictionary.

"Sure," she said, without looking up.

"Benedict Arnold," Micah called.

Ray flashed him a grin as they headed for the door. Outside, the sky was gray and overcast. He judged the temperature to be in the low fifties, at least twenty degrees cooler than the day before. The girls skipped behind him to the car, seeming oblivious to the chilly weather. It wouldn't hurt them to be outside for a few minutes without jackets. What he had to say wouldn't take long.

Ray stopped beside the car but didn't open the door. He turned to face the little girls, his expression serious. "I know what you've been up to."

Both girls stopped dead in their tracks, their eyes as big as silver dollars.

"You joined the Girl Guides to try to get Micah and Patti together, didn't you? Just like you came to the Bait Shop to encourage me to fight for Celeste."

Mia and Rowena looked like they'd been caught cheating on an exam. Both seemed to develop a sudden fascination with their toes. "Yes," Rowena admitted in a small voice.

"But I didn't fall in the water on purpose." Mia looked up at him, her expression earnest.

Ray couldn't keep up the pretense. He stooped to hug both girls. "I know you didn't." He looked each in the eye in turn. "I just have one thing to say about your matchmaking." He paused, then broke into a grin and gave them the thumbs-up sign. "Nice job. I think its working."

"You were teasing us!" Rowena said.

"Just a little. If you'll forgive me, I have a present for each of you. To show my appreciation for all your help." He reached into the car and pulled out two packages wrapped in shiny red foil.

"Do we have to wait till Christmas?" Mia asked.

"Nope, you can open them right now."

Ray watched as the girls tore into their gifts. Rowena's eyes lit up as she pulled out a large, beautifully illustrated book about Native American myths and legends. She immediately began leafing through the pages. "Thank you, Ray," she said.

Mia just stared at her gift. An Annie Leibowitz portrait graced the cover.

"It's the book of photos I told you about. If you keep taking pictures, you'll have a book of your own someday."

"Do you really think so?" Mia hugged the volume to her chest. The radiant expression on her face was all the thanks he needed.

"Thank you Lord for this food, for health and happiness, for friends and family."

As Micah said the blessing, Celeste peeked through downcast lashes at the group assembled around the big mahogany table in the formal dining room. Across from her sat Micah, Patti, and Rowena. Rosa occupied the seat at the head of the table, as befitted the matriarch, and Celeste sat between Ray and Mia. The seat at the other end of the table was conspicuously vacant.

How she wished her father could join them. Not only in body, but in the spirit of love and forgiveness. If she could only make him understand how happy Ray made her, how he'd helped Mia grow in confidence, what joy he'd brought to their lives . . .

". . . and we ask for your guidance for all who are gathered here. Amen."

A chorus of Amens rang out around the table. As the turkey and dressing, the cranberries and sweet potatoes, the tamales and tortillas were passed from hand to hand, Celeste offered a silent prayer of her own. *Thank you, Lord, for Ray Fontana.*

Later, after the dishes had been cleared, the adults lingered over pie and coffee while the little girls squirmed in their chairs. Ray had picked at the delicious Thanksgiving feast, his stomach knotted at the audacity of what he was about to ask.

He didn't deserve Celeste. Deep down inside, he'd always known that. Somehow, he'd been given a second chance at happiness with her and Mia, a daughter he hadn't even known existed. Was it providence? He didn't know for sure, but he wasn't about to let the opportunity slip away from him. Not this time.

"You girls can be excused," Celeste said.

As the little girls scrambled out of their seats, Ray drew a deep breath. "Wait," he said. Mia and Rowena turned questioning eyes on him, as did everyone else at the table.

"I have something to say, and I'd like you to hear it."

The silence was broken by the sound of retreat

ing footsteps. Everyone turned toward the dining room door, where they glimpsed a flash of unnaturally bright red hair before the figure bounded up the stairs two at a time.

"Shifty Sheila." Celeste put a hand over her mouth, as though she wished she could recall the words. "She's the night nurse. I can't imagine what she was doing outside the dining room."

Ray glanced at the faces around him. Patti appeared curious, Micah uneasy. The little girls gaped in wonder at Celeste. Rosa's plump face creased in an expression of disapproval.

Ray's heart sank. A sense of impending doom weighed on him, squeezing the oxygen from his lungs. Something terrible was about to happen. He felt like a fish thrown onto the shore, flopping and gasping for air, unable to alter his destiny.

"Ray?" Celeste touched his hand, her sweet face filled with concern. "Are you all right?"

Ray steeled himself. Whatever lay ahead, he'd come out swinging. If he was quick, strong, and determined, he might still have a chance. He'd play the game the only way he knew how—to win.

He didn't have time for flowery speeches. He pulled the box from his pocket and opened it, revealing a flawless, one-karat marquise-cut diamond ring. "Celeste, will you marry me?"

Celeste gazed at him, elation warring with distress and confusion. This was the moment she'd waited for. She should be ecstatic, but something was terribly wrong. Ray looked more like a warrior preparing for battle than a man asking the woman he loved to become his wife. His dark eyes glittered fiercely and the jagged scar on his forehead leaped to life.

As Celeste hesitated, a voice sounded in the doorway. "Before you answer, I think there are some things you should know."

A collective gasp rose from the group at the dining table. Their attention riveted on the unexpected guest—Dr. Nilson, flanked by the night nurse.

"F-father," Celeste stammered. "What are you doing here?"

Dr. Nilson turned his icy blue stare on his only daughter. "Saving you from making the biggest mistake of your life." His left arm curled uselessly in his lap. He methodically shifted the steel exercise balls against the backdrop of his black velvet robe. With his right hand he pointed at Ray.

"This man, Raymond Fontana, has lied to you from the moment he arrived in Aubrey's Landing. He led you to believe he was a poor but honest mechanic, when in truth, he's a major stockholder and chairman of the board of Native Spirit Boats, a multimillion-dollar corporation."

Celeste looked from her father to Ray. She felt as if she'd been slapped, hard. Tears of hurt and betrayal welled in her eyes.

Ray took her hand. He held her gaze, as if they were the only two people in the room. For a split second, the scene on the hospital patio flashed in her brain, the day he'd adopted Pooch. He'd held her attention the same way, making her feel like they were alone in a crowd. "Is it true?" she asked

"Yes." Ray's voice sounded strong. "I planned to tell you. Call me insecure, but I needed to know that you loved me for myself. The guy you've gotten to know over the last few months. The rest is just window dressing."

Celeste felt her heart go out to the man sitting next to her. How like Ray. On the surface, so sure of himself, but underneath never quite believing he deserved love and acceptance.

"There's more."

Once again, their attention swung to the doorway. Sheila's glance skittered nervously around the room. Evidently, she didn't have the stomach for facing her victims.

Dr. Nilson's gaze never wavered. His old man's voice quivered with righteous wrath.

"Under Fontana's leadership, the board of directors of Native Spirit Boats shut down three factories in this country, putting hundreds of people out of work. The plants were moved to Mexico, where they could obtain cheap labor, without having to pay benefits."

Celeste looked at Ray, hoping for a denial, an explanation, anything to ease the sick feeling in the pit of her stomach. She could almost see the walls going up around him, hear the iron gates clanging shut.

Dr. Nilson leaned slightly forward in his chair, his eyes branding Ray with icy fire. Lifting his good hand, he motioned to Sheila. She handed him a file she'd been hiding behind his chair. Dr. Nilson opened it and withdrew a photo.

A smiling, tuxedoed Ray had his arm around a dark-haired man, also in formal attire. They shared a small, cluttered table with a bored looking blond. The photo appeared to have been taken in a nightclub.

"This is Hector Marquez, leader of the Marquez drug cartel, and a valued customer of Native Spirit Boats. Fontana obtained an exclusive contract for Native Spirit to provide the offshore racing boats Marquez needed to move his product into Florida. With Fontana's help, the cartel was able to outrun any boat in the water, including the Coast Guard and the DEA."

Stricken, Celeste again looked at Ray, hoping her father was wrong. It couldn't be true. This wasn't the Ray she knew. His hooded expression revealed nothing, but the lightning bolt throbbed on his forehead.

"He paid for your OB Center," the doctor said.

Celeste gasped and for the first time, her father's eyes shifted away from Ray. He held her in his steely gaze. "With drug money."

Her emotions were a tangled knot, and right now that knot felt as though it might strangle her. "Is this true?" she whispered. Her eyes pleaded with Ray to say it wasn't.

He looked at her and she thought she caught a glimmer of the Ray she knew and loved. Just as quickly, it was gone, replaced by a cold, unfeeling mask. His lips tilted slightly upward, but the smile held neither warmth nor mirth. Then he shrugged. "It was business, angel."

Celeste felt something die inside her. The bloom of love and hope seemed to shrivel, leaving her dry and aching.

Mia began to sob. Although she didn't understand all that had been said, she apparently sensed the strong emotions and knew something terrible had happened. Celeste took her daughter in her lap. Suddenly, anger filled the void inside her. She glared at Ray with a mother's fury. "Our whole relationship has been a lie. I wish you'd never come here."

Ray rose, tossing the ring box on the table. "You're right. I shouldn't have come back to Aubrey's Landing. I don't belong here, and I never will." He looked at the stricken faces around the table, tenderly touched Mia's cheek and walked out the door. Sheila scurried quickly out of his way, putting the doctor's wheelchair between her and the man she'd helped destroy.

Rowena began to cry in sympathy with Mia. Patti

comforted her while Micah jumped up to follow his brother. Rosa cleared the table, muttering to herself about coyotes in sheep's clothing.

Only Celeste heard the electric whir of her father's wheelchair as he turned toward the elevator. He looked older somehow, worn down by his battle. As she watched, he clutched his chest and slumped to the floor.

Chapter Thirteen

Celeste taped the last box of her father's belongings. In accordance with his will, all the personal effects she didn't want were to be sold, with the profits going to Micah's church. He'd also named Micah the executor of his estate and left him a large amount of cash. It came as quite a surprise to everyone, but life seemed to be full of surprises lately.

She looked around at the bare walls, covered with pale blue watered silk. The house was hers, of course, but for the life of her, she didn't know what to do with it. The old place had a split personality. Downstairs, Rosa had made it warm and homey, while the upstairs, well, it was a living area only her father could love.

She straightened, stretching her lower back and gazed out the window at the gray, gloomy day. It reminded her of the day Ray left, the day her father died. As she watched, a light rain began to fall.

No one had heard from Ray since the day he left Aubrey's Landing. Micah left messages with his secretary and on his home answering machine, to no avail.

He's probably basking in the sun on a Pacific Island. The image of Ray lying on a beach with the buxom blond in the nightclub photo flashed in her brain, but she immediately shoved it aside. It hurt too much.

She ached in a hundred different ways. For her father, whom she'd loved as much as he let her. For Mia, who had retreated into her shell again. And yes, damn it, for herself. Deceived, disappointed, and dumped. When would she ever learn?

Celeste swiped at the tear that rolled down her cheek. She wouldn't go there again. She covered that territory too many times in the past couple of weeks. Ray was gone. Or maybe he'd never really existed, at least not the Ray she thought she knew. Christmas was only two weeks away and she hadn't even bought a tree yet. It was time to pick up the pieces and get on with her life.

Clumping down the stairs, she found Mia in her usual spot by the fireplace with Pooch curled up beside her. The book of photos Ray had given her lay open in her lap.

"Hey, sweet pea." Celeste knelt beside her daughter, who gave her a desultory, "Hi, Mom." Pooch raised his eyes and thumped his tail a couple of times, then gazed back into the flames.

Celeste didn't know which of them had been more devastated by Ray's abrupt departure. Mia and Pooch seemed to take comfort in each other's presence. They'd been inseparable since the day Ray disappeared. Maybe that was why he'd left Pooch on their doorstep with a note asking Mia to take care of him.

Or maybe a mongrel dog didn't fit into the lifestyles of the rich and famous.

"Want to watch a video, sweetie? I brought a couple of your favorite Christmas movies."

Mia turned a listless glance in her direction. "I guess."

"Okay, I'll put this in and go help Rosa finish dinner. Why don't you and Pooch sit over here where you can see better?" Celeste patted the love seat facing the fireplace and television.

She'd tried to tell Mia why Ray left but felt her efforts were painfully inadequate. How do you explain to a seven-year-old why a man you love would suddenly walk out of your life? With Ray's defection and the death of her grandfather, Mia had suffered a double blow. Although Micah had tried to help, Celeste sensed he was struggling with inner demons of his own.

She helped Mia get comfy on the couch, tucking a pillow behind her daughter's shoulders and an old afghan around her legs. Pooch jumped up and rested his head on the little girl's lap. Ordinarily, Celeste would have made him get down, but tonight she didn't have the heart. "Good boy," she said, scratching the bristly hair behind his ear.

"Thanks, Mom." Mia gave her a little smile.

She didn't know if Mia was thanking her for the blanket or letting Pooch stay. Either way, she was grateful. She brushed the hair away from Mia's forehead and kissed her baby soft skin. "I'll call you when dinner's ready."

When Celeste entered the kitchen she found Micah and Rosa huddled over coffee at the table. A delicious aroma wafted from the oven. "Hello, Micah. What brings you here?"

Micah stood. "I was hoping you'd have a few minutes to talk. I don't want to interrupt your dinner." A deep line creased his usually smooth forehead and dark smudges shadowed his eyes. Caught up in her own troubles, she hadn't noticed that Micah had lost weight.

He looks tired, she thought. And worried about something. She opened her mouth to invite him to dinner when Rosa spoke up.

"You eat with us Reverend Micah." It was more a

command than an invitation. Rosa craned her neck at the blond giant who towered over her. "My *chilaquiles con pollo* will make you, how do they say, fat and happy."

"Tortilla casserole with chicken," Celeste translated. "We insist." Micah had been her rock, always available when she needed advice, support, or just an friendly ear. Tonight it looked like he could use a friend.

"All right. Thank you," Micah said. "Although when you hear what I have to say, you may be happy to see me go."

Rosa looked from one to the other, her expression apprehensive. "*Santos,* not again." She crossed herself and started to get up.

Micah put a hand on her shoulder. "Stay, Rosa. Please."

Celeste sank into the chair next to Rosa, as a sense of unease tightened her chest. *Bad luck comes in threes.* An icy fear gripped her. "Has something happened to Ray?"

Micah shook his head. "No, no. At least, not as far as I know. I still haven't heard from him."

Thank God, Celeste thought. She'd rather imagine Ray on a beach with a hundred bikini-clad bimbos than have any harm come to him. No matter how much he'd hurt her, she still loved him. There was no sense in denying it. Sometimes, at night, when the house was still, she missed him so much she thought the pain might tear her to pieces.

Micah began to pace, covering the distance between the dining table and the sink in three long strides. Suddenly, he wheeled in their direction. "Do you know why your father named me executor of his estate?" he asked.

She'd never seen Micah this agitated. Instinctively, she reached for Rosa's hand under the table. "I assumed it was because he didn't have much confidence in my business sense. Father thought I was too naive and trusting." She paused as bittersweet memories seeped into her consciousness. "Maybe he was right."

"Wrong." Micah stopped pacing. He stared at her with such intensity, it was all Celeste could do not to flinch. She felt Rosa give her hand a reassuring squeeze.

Suddenly all the fire seemed to go out of him. He sighed and sat down in the chair, cradling his coffee cup. "Leander Nilson was wrong about a lot of things. He thought he took his secret to the grave with him. But I know. I've known for years and I've been just as wrong to keep silent." He stared moodily into his coffee, lost for the moment in his own thoughts.

Celeste and Rosa exchanged a glance. What had happened to calm, even-tempered, gentle Micah?

This tormented soul bore little resemblance to the man they knew and loved. Tentatively, Celeste reached out a hand. "Why don't you just start at the beginning?"

"I'll get some more coffee," Rosa said. She brought another cup for Celeste and a carton of milk from the refrigerator. She refilled her cup and Micah's, then poured three fingers of coffee in the third cup. Celeste added an equal amount of milk and two lumps of sugar.

She'd learned to drink coffee that way from her father. One of her earliest memories was sipping a teaspoon of milk and sugar-laced coffee from his cup. How precious that small gift had seemed to her. The faint strains of Christmas music filtered in from the living room as the grandfather clock struck six. The gentle patter of rain filled the quiet corners of the room.

"Years ago, my mother worked her way out West with a girlfriend," Micah began. "They drove an old rattletrap car all the way from Chicago, stopping when they ran out of money to waitress or clean motel rooms. They made it as far as Aubrey's Landing before the car gave out completely. Mom and her friend got jobs at Betty's Diner. The friend hung around just long enough to earn bus fare to the coast, but Mom stayed."

He looked up at Rosa and Celeste, his expression pained. "She met someone. A young man from a prominent family. I guess it was love at first sight. At least, that's what she told me. They dated for a while but kept their relationship secret. Then Mom got pregnant."

Celeste felt as though she couldn't breathe. An unbearable heaviness lodged in her chest. She didn't dare look at Rosa, for fear she'd find her suspicion confirmed in the older woman's eyes. "But they didn't get married."

Micah shook his head. "His parents wouldn't have approved. He offered to pay for an abortion, or even help support her and the baby on his meager student's income. Mom was too proud to accept anything less than total commitment. She married Al Fontana, and as far as everyone in Aubrey's Landing knows, he's my father." Micah paused, his eyes pleading for understanding. "But my real father, my biological father is . . ."

"Leander Nilson." For a moment she could only stare at him in wonder. How could she have been so blind? He had her height, her coloring, even the same long, slender fingers. Micah was her brother.

Slowly she walked around the table, then knelt to put her arms around him. She pressed her face against his chest, her tears dampening the soft flannel shirt. "Why didn't you tell me?"

Micah folded her in a warm embrace. "Mom told me on her deathbed. I promised her I'd give Leander the chance to tell me himself. She always be-

lieved he would someday. I guess I hoped for a reconciliation too, but that opportunity has passed.
The closest he came to acknowledging me was
leaving me part of his estate, and making me the
executor of his will."

Celeste remained silent. So many things made
sense now. Her father's emotional distance, his de-
votion to his work. She looked up to see that
Micah's cheeks were damp with tears. "Your
mother was the love of his life," she said. "When he
lost her, he never allowed himself to feel again."
Suddenly, another thought struck her. "But why did
he hate Ray so much?"

Micah helped her to her feet. She pulled a chair
around the table and sat beside him, not wanting to
miss a moment's closeness.

"I think Ray reminded him of Alonso, who he
blamed for ruining my mother's life. Mom told me
Dr. Nilson tried to get her to divorce Al. He offered
her money to help raise me but she wouldn't accept
it. Juleska was unbending in her belief in honesty
and commitment."

"It's too bad Father didn't share her values." Celeste couldn't keep the note of censure from her
voice.

Rosa jumped up, startling both of them. "I'll be
right back," she said.

As the kitchen door swung closed, Micah turned
to Celeste. "He was young. He carried his family's

hopes on his shoulders. They expected him to become a doctor, marry the right girl, take his place in society. Later he had you and your mother to consider."

"And his reputation." She felt sure her father had never forgiven himself for abandoning the woman he loved and their infant son. But then, he'd never been able admit he was wrong, either. Or make amends for his mistake. He'd kept his shame and guilt locked inside, where it had eaten away at him until he'd lost the ability to express his feelings in a healthy way.

"Can you forgive me?"

It was as though Micah had read her thoughts. "Of course," she said, taking his hand. "You honored your mother's dying request. I wouldn't have expected you to do anything less."

"I tried to keep in contact with you over the years, to help out when I could," Micah said.

"And so did your papa." Rosa stood at the kitchen door, clutching a sheaf of papers to her chest. "I found these when I was helping Celestina." She handed them to Celeste.

"Riverside Theological Seminary," Celeste read. "They look like receipts."

"Can I see those?" Micah took the papers from her. "They are receipts. From the years I attended seminary."

Rosa nodded. "I didn't understand at first. Then I forgot about them. There were so many papers."

Micah turned disbelieving eyes on the two women. "He paid my way through seminary." He spoke in a tone of quiet amazement. "I wouldn't be surprised if he had a hand in my living with Reverend Simpson too."

Rosa went to the stove to check her *chilaguiles*. She retrieved a pair of hot pads and pulled the casserole from the oven. When she turned toward them again, her brown eyes were soft, her voice gentle. "Your papa, he was a good man. He did the best he could."

Celeste and Micah sat quietly for a moment, stunned by the night's revelations. Finally, Micah spoke. "Perhaps, in the end, that's all any of us can do."

It was business, angel.
I wish you'd never come back to Aubrey's Landing.
He did the best he could.

Celeste spent a sleepless night, replaying the events of the recent past in her mind. She couldn't believe it had been only two weeks since Ray left. So much had happened, she felt as if her whole world had been turned upside down.

Was she wrong to be so hard on Ray? That night at the dinner table, he'd proposed to her. If things had been different, they might be engaged now.

She sat up in bed and pounded the pillow a couple of times. No, damn it, it wouldn't have worked.

She'd endured one marriage based on a lie and swore she'd never do it again.

But she loved Ray. And she hadn't exactly been honest either.

No matter how she twisted and turned, she couldn't escape the cruel daggers of conscience. She'd condemned Ray without even giving him the chance to explain.

Maybe she had more of her father in her than she liked to admit.

Chapter Fourteen

Celeste took a final look around before her guests arrived. The Christmas tree occupied one corner of the living room with brightly wrapped presents piled underneath. A CD featuring Celtic harp music played softly in the background and the house smelled like pine needles and freshly baked cookies.

She and Mia spent the day baking, a Christmas Eve tradition they'd enjoyed since Mia was a toddler. Although Celeste had tried to make the occasion happy, she couldn't help feeling it had fallen flat.

Who was she kidding? The whole season had fallen flat without Ray. They'd become so accustomed to him living next door, banging away at his house, whistling show tunes and incinerating steaks on the barbecue. Even when he wasn't spending time with them, the sounds and the scents emanating from his house had become part of the fabric of their lives. And the sight of him, well, that never failed to quicken her pulse. She realized now that she'd counted on Ray's presence. When he was living next door she felt safe and loved.

She tried to reach him after her talk with Micah but his home phone was disconnected. A call to Native Spirit Boats had earned her the terse message that Mr. Fontana no longer worked there. She was left with the receiver dangling from her hand and a dial tone ringing in her ear.

Where on earth had he gone? she wondered for the millionth time. The image of a tropical island and bikini-clad blond popped into her mind but she resolutely pushed it away. Ray would resurface when he was ready, Micah said. She'd just have to be patient.

With a sigh, she circled the living room, picking up a coloring book and crayons from the coffee table and a fat plastic hamburger from underneath. She placed the chew toy on the round cedar-filled pillow they'd bought for Pooch as an early Christmas present. It looked like their scruffy houseguest might be with them for quite a while.

The sound of voices on the front porch shook her out of her doldrums. Pooch's enthusiastic woofs announced Rosa's arrival with treats for all, including a bone for her favorite dog. Celeste crossed quickly to the front door and greeted her mamacita with a hug.

Looking past Rosa, she saw that Mia held a platter containing a *Rosca de los Reyes,* Three Kings Bread. Baked in a ring and studded with jewels of candied fruit and nuts, the confection resembled a royal crown. Mexican families traditionally ate the bread on January 6th to celebrate the coming of the three wise men. She cocked an eyebrow at Rosa.

"I know." The older woman handed her a plastic bag filled with fresh, warm tamales. "It's not Twelfth Night yet but Mia asked me to bake it early this year. Isn't that right, my little sparrow?"

Mia nodded, her eyes shining. She looked proud and a bit awed by the responsibility of carrying the Three Kings Bread. Behind her Pooch grinned around a juicy bone. The little procession followed Celeste into the house.

Patti and Rowena arrived a short time later. They planned to share a light dinner and attend the Christmas Eve service at church. It would be the first year the girls were allowed to stay up for the ten o'clock service. They left the grown-ups to their own devices and went into Mia's room to play.

Celeste sensed a conspiracy in the air. The girls were too quiet, and she saw them exchange more than one meaningful glance. Even Rosa seemed to be in on it. No matter, Mia looked happier than she'd been in weeks. In fact she looked—Celeste fumbled for the right adjective—hopeful. Yes, that was it. If Mia's secret had that effect on her, then let her keep it. It warmed Celeste's heart to hear her giggling again.

Micah phoned just before dinner to say he'd been summoned for an emergency. "I guess that's what life will be like as preacher's wife," Celeste teased.

To her surprise, Patti didn't come back with a tart reply. In fact, the irreverent blond blushed and smiled shyly.

So that's how it is. She knew Patti and Micah had been seeing a lot each other lately, but she'd been too wrapped up in her misery to realize just how serious their relationship had become. She gave her friend a quick hug. She was happy for Patti and Micah, truly happy, but somehow their good fortune left her feeling lower than Pooch's well-chewed plastic burger.

After dinner Rosa cut pieces of the Three Kings Bread for everyone. The little girls wiggled with excitement. They all took small bites, knowing a tiny ceramic doll was hidden in one of the slices.

"I got it!" Mia shouted. "I got the Three Kings doll."

Rosa nodded gravely. "The kings bring *buena suerte,* good luck. Make a wish, Mia."

Mia closed her eyes. Her forehead puckered in

concentration. "There." She opened her eyes and her little face glowed with pleasure. "I hope it comes true."

"So do I, sweetheart," said Celeste. *So do I.*

She scooped Mia out of the car and carried her onto the front porch. It was more habit than hope that directed her gaze next door. Ray's house was quiet and dark.

He'd been gone for a month now, but the house hadn't been listed with a realtor yet. Maybe that meant he intended to return. *And maybe someday pigs would fly.*

She fumbled in her purse for keys. Ray had walked out of her life once before. Why should she believe he wouldn't do it again? Especially since she'd told him she wished he had never come back.

She wasn't being fair. Ray had never intentionally hurt her or Mia. The Ray she had gotten to know was kind and courageous, sensitive and caring.

But what about the other Ray, the one who closed factories, and did business with drug lords? The man who made a profit off others' misery.

Who was the real Ray Fontana?

Inside, she tucked Mia into bed. As she started to leave, the picture of herself and Ray standing in front of the graffiti-scrawled fireplace caught her eye. It had been taken the day they toured his house and still occupied a prominent place on Mia's dresser. She picked it up for a closer look.

She was gazing at him with such a goofy expression on her face. Even then, although she'd have rather eaten dirt than admit it, she was in love with him.

Celeste shook her head. She never had a chance. The minute Ray walked into her life, she'd been hooked. Turning toward the bed, she saw Mia watching her.

"You look sad, Mama."

Celeste blinked back the tears that burned her eyelids. "I'm okay, baby. It's just an emotional time of year."

Mia continued to study her with somber blue-gray eyes. "He's coming back, Mom. I know he is. I wished for it on the Three Kings Cake."

Celeste didn't know what to say. She couldn't bear to dash the little girl's hopes on Christmas Eve. She smoothed Mia's hair away from her forehead. "Go to sleep, sweetie. You'll want to get up early to see what Santa brought."

Mia snuggled down into the covers and hugged her favorite stuffed rabbit. "Good night, Mom. Merry Christmas."

"Merry Christmas, sugarplum."

Although it was almost midnight, she didn't feel sleepy yet. She brushed her teeth, scrubbed her face clean of makeup and put on her most comfortable nightgown and an ancient chenille robe. Maybe if she went outside, she'd see a jolly fat man flying across the sky. She smiled wistfully at her reflection in the bathroom mirror. She could use a miracle this Christmas Eve.

The night was clear and mild. As she padded across the front porch in the fluffy slippers Mia had given her last Christmas, a million stars sparkled in the night sky. *Like the jewels in a king's crown,* Celeste thought.

Thunk. The sound came from the house next door. Burglars often targeted vacant homes, and Ray had left all his belongings behind. She pulled her robe closer around her and crept back against the house, glancing around for a weapon.

Not a rock or baseball bat in sight. *Of course there's no baseball bat. We don't play baseball.* Celeste did a mental head whack, then took off one of her slippers. *If all else fails I can throw it at him,* she thought.

She didn't have to wait long. A man ambled down the steps with a dancer's grace. Black hair gleamed in the distant glow of a streetlight. He crossed the yard and stood on the grass below her. "Hello, angel."

Celeste clutched the porch rail. Her heart pounded so hard she thought it might leap out of her chest. "Ray? Is it really you?"

"Yes, its me."

"I—I thought you were a burglar."

Ray's dark eyes glinted with amusement. "Did you plan to tickle me to death?"

She looked down at the fuzzy pink slipper she still clutched. Hurriedly, she replaced it on her foot. "No, of course not. I planned to call nine-one-one. I was just going to throw it at you . . . him . . . the burglar . . . if he tried to attack me." She felt ridiculous standing there in her threadbare robe and big cotton candy slippers. "What are you doing here?" she asked.

"I had some unfinished business. Can we talk for a few minutes?"

Celeste wanted to throw herself into Ray's arms and tell him she loved him. She wanted to beg him to stay. Instead, she pointed at two chairs on her front porch and said, "Sure, come on up."

Instinctively, she touched the medallion Rosa had given her long ago. If ever she'd needed a boost of faith and confidence, it was now.

Ray took one chair while she settled into the other. She folded her hands in her lap to keep them from trembling. Ray appeared calm but she noticed that he sat slightly forward in his seat with one foot in front of the other. *The fighter's stance.*

"Mia told me you were coming back. She wished for you on the Three Kings Cake," she said.

Ray looked pained. "I'm sorry I left so suddenly. When your father told you about my business dealings, and I saw the look on your face, I felt I didn't belong here."

"I never should have said—"

Ray stopped her. "Please. I don't blame you for being upset. In a way, your father did me a favor. He held up a mirror and showed me the sorry excuse for a human being I'd become.

"I can't change what I've done, or justify it. Businesses move their manufacturing plants to Mexico or overseas every day but that doesn't make it right.

"For the record, I want you to know that Native Spirit also sold their fastest offshore racing boats to the Coast Guard and the Drug Enforcement Administration." He grinned fiercely in the darkness. "We evened the odds and made a tidy profit."

She felt a chill seep into her bones. Drawing her feet under her, she wrapped her arms around her body and waited for Ray to continue. She'd promised herself she wouldn't judge him again. The least she could do was hear him out.

"Life was a game, angel, and I played to win. Then I came back to Aubrey's Landing and everything changed. I learned that people matter, relationships, family, friends. Somehow, I lost touch with that."

She wanted to comfort him, to tell him that

everything would be all right, but she couldn't get the words past the lump in her throat.

"I sold my shares in Native Spirit Boats," Ray continued. "I could retire on the profit and live comfortably for rest of my life, but somehow I can't see myself sitting on the front porch with my feet up."

Celeste smiled through her tears. The thought of Ray leading a sedentary life was like expecting a puma to be content in a cage. "What will you do?" she asked.

Ray leaned forward a little more. His eyes shone with enthusiasm. "I want to start a Boys and Girls Ranch in Aubrey's Landing, to give back some of the good things I received. And this time, I'm not just going to throw money at the problem. I plan to work with the kids. Who knows, I may be able to keep a few of them from making the same mistakes I did."

But what about me? a voice inside her cried. Where do I fit into your plans? She wanted him to say he loved her so much he couldn't possibly live without her, but it seemed he had other issues to resolve first. She chided herself for being selfish and immature. "That's wonderful, Ray. Does Micah know about your plans?"

"I called him from the airport this evening. He came to pick me up and we had a long talk. He told me your father died. I'm sorry."

Celeste nodded. The lump in her throat had grown to the size of a golf ball.

"He also told me Leander was his father. It made such perfect sense, I'm amazed I never figured it out. When Dr. Nilson came to my mother's funeral, I thought he came to taunt me. I know now that he grieved for her."

Celeste wiped the tears from her eyes. "Sometimes the hardest mysteries to solve are the ones right under your nose."

They sat in silence for a moment. Celeste peered at Ray from under her lashes. He seemed tense, as though he were poised to step into the ring. The shadowed porch accentuated the planes and angles of his warrior's face.

"I don't expect you to forgive me," he said. "Even if you don't want me for a life partner, I'd like to be a father to Mia. Maybe in time, when I prove to you that I've changed, we could start seeing each other again. I love you, Celeste. I've always loved you."

They were the words she longed for, the words she'd waited to hear. She felt as if she were dreaming and was afraid if she moved too quickly she'd wake up. Slowly, tentatively, she stood and faced him. "I love you too."

In a quick, graceful movement he took her in his arms. His hard body pressed against her, solid and reassuring. She clung to him as he covered her face with kisses. "Can you forgive me?" he whispered in a voice rough with emotion.

"I think a better question is, can you forgive me?" She leaned back to gaze into his dark eyes.

"What for?" he asked.

"For doubting you and my instincts. For forgetting that the man I know and love is the real Ray Fontana."

In answer, he hugged her closer.

"Ray?" she squeaked.

"Yes?"

"I can't breathe."

He laughed and let her go.

"Besides, I have to get something." Hiking her long gown and robe around her knees, Celeste sprinted into the house.

A few moments later, she returned with a small box. "You asked me a question at Thanksgiving dinner that I never got a chance to answer. Do you think we could replay that scene, without the interruption?"

Ray looked like a little boy who'd awakened on Christmas morning to find everything he ever wished for under the tree. He knelt in front of her, then slipped the ring on her finger. His dark eyes glowed with emotion. "Will you marry me?" he asked. "Do you love me enough to grow old with me? Will you give me a second chance?"

She caressed his face with the hand that bore

his ring. "Oh, yes," she said. "I do. And I will. Always."

He stood and she melted against him. Lifting her gaze to the heavens, she saw a shooting star streak across the sky.

"*Que milagro,*" she murmured. "What a miracle."